A SEXY THING

BOOK #8, THE BENT ZEALOTS

AN MM-MC ROMANCE

THEY DO NOT APOLOGIZE FOR A DAMNED THING.

VAN. Revenge for the death of my lover led me west, out of the Appalachian holler where meth-making defined me. I was not that backwoods addict but a clean member of a motorcycle club where violence and mayhem prevailed. My only outlet was cruising the dating apps, and yes, catfishing juicy hunks under a fake profile. Some sleazery just never vanishes. But I was trying.

Hunt. As an astrophysicist and family man, I was seemingly living the good life. But the persona I'd kept hidden for decades insisted on bursting forth. I needed to handle the crazy, so I came out to my wife and children. A heart attack showed me the path, and it led directly to the loving arms of Van Rossi, a down-to-earth fellow hillbilly. His rustic persona brought out the lusty, experimental side of me, and I'd follow him to any jackoff club at the end of the earth.

Van. Dr. Mountjoy is beyond my redneck reach. I loathe myself for scamming such an upstanding academic—with such upstanding equipment. My stunning archangel has dropped from heaven just for me, and I don't deserve him. And when the Society's Baggers come to blast the Bent Zealots MC, Hunt will see the real me. I'm not even brave enough to follow through on my revenge. How can this beautiful saint see anything in me at all? I have my whole life to apologize for, but he doesn't need to apologize for a fucking thing.

Publisher's Note: This book is not for the faint of heart. It contains scenes of graphic gay sex, illegal doings, consensual bondage and discipline, forced seduction, catfishing, rimming, teabagging, jackoff clubs, themes of Daddy dominance, and violence in general. It's a full-length novel of 60,000 words. There is no cheating or cliffhangers, and there are HEAs for all. These are standalone books and can be read out of order.

LAYLA
ROMANCE NOVELIST
WOLFE

A SEXY THING

Book #8, The Bent Zealots

An MM-MC Romance

CHAPTER ONE

Van Rossi

We drove in formation, Tyrone and Jackie riding point.

We cruised like a swarm of murder hornets, our rides so close together we skimmed each other's knees, grazing side mirrors, choking on exhaust. Four of us rode on this run, but the Society's Bag MC was accustomed to doing everything in a pack. I was the peon, the Prospect, so I rode sweep, sometimes known as tail runner. Normally this would be a very experienced guy, but I was the only lackey, so it fell to me.

I was not a very experienced guy.

I lived in constant paranoia, examining my every action. *Did I make them suspicious, did I jump, or not jump enough? Did I say something to give myself away?* I was a fraud, a complete imposter, and we were going on a run to collect some meth a guy named Putrid owed us. Tyrone Shoelaces had ordered me to bring my Beretta, to separate the loaded magazine in case pigs stopped us. Tyrone was high as a Georgia pine, hands shaking, teeth rotting. Seventy miles an hour and under the darkened, starry bowl of the desert sky, I knew Tyrone was blind at night. Still, he rode point.

Routes 40 and 95 skirted the Dead Mountains Wilderness Area. It was dead, all right, to morons who knew nothing of nature, like these jackwads. A nature-loving Tar Heel such as myself could wander these hills endlessly, whipping past the creosote bushes with lemon yellow flowers, dodging jackrabbits and kangaroo squirrels. I'd soak in the hot springs, the shadows of golden eagles peppering my face. Well, before I became Tyrone's slave that is.

I went on runs for him, gathering lottery tickets and McDonald's. I was Chief Pooper Scooper when his untrained dog shit on his living room floor, or in the middle of our Jefferson's clubhouse. At three in the morning I'd be ordered to Taco Hell for tacos minus salsa, burritos with only red beans, the rice on the side. I'd have to go back and exchange the food if there was a slight variation. Exhausted, my entire skeleton creaking and aching, I'd lean against the wall next to the AK-47s as Tyrone staggered in and out in a crank-fueled trance, eyeballs like bowling balls. My job was to inventory the weapons and drugs. I had to report down to the brass knuckles, hoods, and nooses.

Forced to join in drinking contests and being thwacked in the legs with pool sticks during friendly games made it a painful existence. If I shot pool too well I showed disrespect. But if I scratched, I needed to be lectured. It was a lose-lose existence, and I was Tyrone Shoelace's human punching bag. He moved like a Rock 'Em Sock 'Em robot on speed, *pow pow pow.*

Can you tell I did not like the man? I knew better to ask where we were going, but we passed a moonlit sign telling me this was Goffs, California, established 1883, pop 23. We zoomed past the schoolhouse—more like a private house with a sign—a rusted Chevy truck, and the Flywheel Café. I was so fatigued the scene skipped like those old films full of holes. But I persisted, my jaw set, my hands numb from my handlebar's vibrations.

We roared as one unit up to a shack. The others swaggered to the front door as if they owned the place. In a way, they did. This area used to be Society's Bag turf. They were run out of town by another club. From Goffs to Zzyzx—yes, a real town—and sweeping down to the big city Barstow, that was all Bag turf, and had been for ten years. Now? We barely held onto our home base of Needles, a shitshow nobody wanted anyway. We were looking to expand.

The meth dealer, Putrid, lived up to his name. He welcomed us into his ramshackle abode that reminded me of west of Laurinburg, North Carolina, out in the Appalachians somewhere. The house reeked of fertilizer and that dental stink I knew was the half-pound of meth sitting on the kitchen counter. Tyrone hovered his cigarette lighter over the crystalline shards, then took a pinkie finger full of the stuff, as if he were some connoisseur. He snorted, and I could tell his nose was already pre-packed with something else. His rubbery jowls shuddered, and he nodded once with approval.

Putrid started weighing it on the scale set out like he'd been baking. "My old lady is being stalked by her ex. Can you mess him up?"

Tyrone cocked his head with professional acumen. "Smoke him?"

Putrid's lip got snagged on a tooth. "Maybe just scare him."

Jackie Daytona, the Sergeant-at-Arms, was the man for this. "We could cut his limbs off one by one. Or mummify him alive."

The third man, a doofus name of Crosley Shelvador, said, "He said scare, not kill. How about cover him in meat sauce and throw him in a cage with a hungry tiger?"

Tyrone frowned. "Where we gonna find a tiger?"

Cowed, Crosley shrugged. It didn't stop him from making more suggestions. "We could give him paper cuts everywhere."

Tyrone said, "I was thinking more like tie his wrists and ankles to ropes attached to four different horses."

Jackie pointed with approval. "Drawing and quartering." I always thought of Jackie as more sophisticated than the others. He proved it by knowing this. "How about make him walk into a bee farm without a suit?"

I could see Putrid becoming agitated at these violent ideas, so I pulled a wad of cash from my cut pocket. "One G, agreed-upon price," I reminded him. It was a shyster price for the meth, but it was the deal. Tyrone wandered back into the living room as we concluded our business.

"You can extract ricin from castor beans," I suggested. I had done that once. I considered myself a sort of chemist.

"That would kill him," Jackie said. "How about putting him into a room with only a sandpaper conveyor belt for a floor?"

I said, "Inject a syringe full of craft glue and paper into his heart." I knew about this, unfortunately, because it'd been done to a friend of mine back home. I'd lived a hard life, and it hadn't gotten any easier. Out of the frying pan and into the fire. It was just my personality, maybe, my inner self at work dictating my life's path. And it was always seamy, illegal, and downright gone to seed.

"Listen," said Putrid, shoving the meth at me. "Maybe never mind about the stalker. He's not that bad. Here. Thanks for coming by. I'll see you later."

We shuffled into the living room. Tyrone, wasting no time, was making out with a bony, buzzed girl on the couch.

"Hey, Ty," said Jackie Daytona. "We'd better blaze if we want to make it back in time for the Lions Club crab feed."

Yup, that's what we were doing that night. A club of wasted, delirious, destructive men crashed a Lions Club in Needles because we wanted to show the community how helpful we could be. I'd participated in some Toys for Tots runs where we actually gave most, or some of the proceeds to the tots. But the Lions Club? Last time, a brainless Tyrone had elbowed aside the DJ to blast the same Dying Fetus CD over and over while another member, George Zip, passed out face first in the buffet. True, the rest of the guys including me were whipping some Lion wives around the dance floor. I had a crab leg sticking out of my cut pocket. The wives didn't seem to mind, but I'm sure the husbands did. One of them coldcocked poor George Zip in the men's room. That didn't mean we left though.

Tyrone stood, dragging the girl with him. "They gonna have melted butter?"

Jackie shrugged. "Sure. Why not? Or we could bring our own, in like a fondue pot."

"I'll find one," I offered, like a robot.

Tyrone sucked on the girl's mouth a bit more, then peeled her from his arms and flung her to the floor.

She had no legs. Stumps waved from the hem of her short skirt. I'd seen enough of that in my time in the hollers, and I automatically stepped forward to lend her a helping hand.

But Tyrone stopped me. "Van," he reminded me. "You work for me."

"Yes, sir," I replied.

Were all Prospects in other MCs treated like this? I felt like a sullen kid kicking rocks as we made our way to our rides. I was surprised Tyrone didn't order me to give him twenty for my rudeness in wanting to help the disabled girl. Hell, I had to carry a survival kit of condoms—for the members, not myself—tampons to blot blood from bullet wounds, bootlaces, and Norco for Jackie's bad back. There were many days I wondered how long I could maintain this farce, playing this subservient role. *I need to just pop off Tyrone Shoelaces and Jackie Daytona.* What was I waiting for?

I looked forward to returning to our clubhouse. I'd been living there, since I had no time to get a job, and rent was free. I had a windowless room near the kitchen, as would befit any slimy Prospect. There was an Allman Brothers poster on the wall, and I added a Queen one of my own—not framed, just tacked. There. I had decorated. It was my room now. Apparently Crosley Shelvador had committed some fully-patched crime such as discussing club business outside of the club or letting someone else wear his cut, because he was stuck down the hall, too. The rest of the men—Prez, Veep, Sergeant-at-Arms, Treasurer—all lived in their own decent condos. I knew, because I spent my days shuttling back and forth between them, doing their bidding.

Not a mile from Jefferson's, fucking Tyrone waved us in a different direction. *Bless his heart.* He wanted to go stir up yet more trouble. I knew where we were headed, a bar another riding club inhabited. A riding club wasn't a one percent club, just hobbyists who got together on the weekend in order to play darts and ride their rice rockets. We scoffed at them, called them wannabes, outsiders. Hell, they had little microphones inside their helmets so they could talk to each other as they rode. We just had to gesture. And most of us didn't even wear lids, maybe just skullcaps.

What the fuck now? I had a serious craving to log onto my laptop. I was probably too afraid of an IRL hookup, but I wanted to at least chat with non-thug humans. I didn't like to video chat with my naturally curly hair bashed in on one side from my skullcap and lid, but DMing was almost as good.

I knew I could easily put a stop to this never-ending cycle of violence. But I'd somehow along the way been caught up with the drama. Life in the holler, believe it or not, had a certain dramatic sheen to it. Someone's meth operation blew up. Someone fucked someone else's woman. As white trash as we were, there was still room for soap operas. Having moved all the way across the country, I found myself mired in a typical holler tragedy.

There were so many Kawasakis and Yamahas out front, we had to park before an old-timey drugstore. With its Rexall sign, faded *People* magazines, and Budweiser beer signs, it made me feel at home. Except Tyrone angrily spat out words.

"That jagov in there, Bob Frost, he knocked over George's ride the other day in a Target parking lot."

"You're fucking kidding me," said Jackie. "Why the fuck would he do something like that?"

"Said it was an accident when he parked next to him. But what the fuck, we want those outsiders off our turf anyway. What do you say?"

Crosley's eyebrows shot up with glee. "I say fuck *yeah!*" Sometimes I wondered where Crosley was from. He acted like a six foot kid from the suburbs. He'd look at home with an elf's hat on.

"Yeah, why not?" I said, trying to inject my voice with enthusiasm.

Tyrone asked Jackie, "You up for it?" I knew he was checking on Jackie's back. Something to do with his discs, probably messed up in a bar fight.

Jackie shrugged too, prompting me to open my survival kit and tap three Norco from the bottle. I palmed them to Jackie. "Why not? Looks like only eight guys in there."

Crosley said, "I've got my steel nun chucks." He removed them from his saddlebags to prove it, swinging them too near Tyrone's rearview mirror. They *were* steel, too—not even wood like most of them. Tyrone snatched them from him.

I started to say, "I've got my—" but Jackie grabbed my brass knuckles from me.

That was good enough for Tyrone. "Come on!" he urged, swaggering up the sidewalk, snapping the nun chucks between his fists. This was one time it was good to bring up the rear. Still, I really had no fear of these Speedy Bastards, or whatever tough moniker they used. I pressed weights in what I liked to call the "weight room" at Jefferson's. It was part of the New Me. I always told myself I'd seen much worse. And I probably had. So we stormed up there like the bar was the complaint desk, Tyrone even kicking in the swinging door.

I elbowed aside a few guys smoking cigarettes, and they didn't protest. That was the damn thing about being a Society's Bagger—everyone seemed to think they deserved our treatment. And so they probably did, I told myself whenever I kicked the ass of strangers. This place clamored with drinkers, death metal booming from speakers on high. Tyrone targeted a pool player, his square body crammed into tight jeans, his shirt riding high on his gut. In other words, like any rube I associated with in the holler. His wintry beard was unkempt and wild.

Tyrone spit on the floor. This got Bob Frost's attention. He looked up from the table, like, "Yes? Can I help you?" Of course he didn't recognize Tyrone, as only George Zip had been in the Target parking lot—if anyone was. George Zip could've easily fabricated that incident to start a turf war. Tyrone jabbed a stiff forefinger into his own cut. "Recognize *these* patches?" he yelled.

Bob squinted to see, and when he came closer Tyrone just sucker-punched him, jabbing him so violently square on his chin with the nun chucks the guy flew backward onto the pool table with an abrasive *crack*. Only his pool partner dared step forward to defend the guy, and Jackie Daytona took him on. Jackie swung a tight uppercut to the Speedy Bastard's jaw, his brass knuckles glinting. Because Jackie was slighter than Tyrone—and his bad back probably didn't help—the blow only stunned the hefty Bastard, and he thwacked Jackie over the skull with his pool cue.

It's on. As Jackie collapsed like a lawn chair, I stepped into the role of suave defender. Blocking the Bastard's blow with my forearm, I kneed him in the groin. He went to his knees in prayer, but I wasn't done. I had to make it look good to my brothers in arms. So I wrenched a big handful of the Kawasaki-riding Bastard's T-shirt, pummeling his face mercilessly. Drops of blood were really flying, like a squeezed lemon. Bob Frost tried to get off the table, but instantly received a series of hooks and jabs from both Tyrone and a recovered Jackie.

Crosley Shelvador, meanwhile, took on every mother and his brother. Crosley was the bully of the beach, lifting men on high like a wrestler, and tossing them to the mat. Only in this case the floor was already swimming in beer and broken glass. My victim thrashed to and fro as I dragged him toward an EXIT sign. His Bastard brothers shouted threats, but no one touched me. This was a riding club, not a one percent motorcycle club. They weren't accustomed to shit like this.

The empty alley was only populated with a lone, silent dumpster. The Bastard squirmed wildly, raked my forearms with his nails, and generally exuded blood and sweat. But I was there to save him. I tossed him, and he rolled toward the dumpster.

"Get out," I advised, and he did.

He bounded away like a football in play, looking over his shoulder at me, never stopping.

I sighed and absently patted my stomach. I needed several long, large gulps of air to steel myself for the foul bar. The place looked like a hurricane had blown through, furniture scattered everywhere, people rolling on pool balls. Shards of glass sparkled in Crosley's hair while he held a Bastard down, just so Tyrone could kick his head. Blood splashed from my knuckles when I backhanded Tyrone. Who cared? I was the one who'd be stuck handwashing the blood from his rockers on his cut.

"Hey, Prez," I bellowed. "What about that crab feed?"

Tyrone stood erect, eyes blinking, panting. "That's right," he seemed to say. I couldn't tell, the clamor in the room was so deafening.

I waved an arm in the direction of the front door. "Come on."

Tyrone wrenched Jackie's sleeve. Jackie appeared relieved to drop the guy he'd been thrashing. Tyrone allowed Crosley one last body to toss onto the bar before joining us with a grin, as though he'd just gotten off a Ferris wheel.

It had been a one-sided fight, really. Those poor Bastards never stood a chance. We were a lean, mean, ass-kicking machine.

Except maybe Jackie. I had the nerve to brush his cut with my fingertips as we strode to our rides, flipping up our collars like a gang in *West Side Story*. "Hey, why don't you go get surgery for your back?"

Jackie shivered, flapping his lips. He shook his hands back and forth like they'd been about to fall asleep. "It's too expensive and creepy. Way too many of the surgeries fail. I just want them to make Norco stronger, or I'm moving onto morphine or fentanyl." He took beyond the max Norco allowed per day. He always bitched about the FDA regulating it, the Chinese controlling it.

"Yeah," I agreed. "Fucking FDA needs to come to the party."

"One of these days," said Jackie, "I'm going to *smoke* the FDA."

"Hey," I called to Jackie as I flung a leg over the saddle of my Springer Softail. "We should clean up before the crab feed. My knuckles are bleeding."

Tyrone tried to give me a thumbs up, but couldn't form that gesture with his injured hand. "Good going, Van Halen." That was his witty name for me. "I think I'll skip the crab feed and go home. Kicking those asses gave me a big appetite."

Uh-oh. I mentally filled Tyrone's Taco Hell order—I had brussels sprouts and organic ground beef in the fridge back at Jefferson's. With my new workout regime, I avoided junk food.

Jackie Daytona was puffed up with the current victory. "Next, we head to Lake Havasu and take over Bent Zealots turf." The Bent Zealots were another one percent club of mostly gay men. Need I add that Society's Bag loathed them even more than straight bikers?

Tyrone laughed casually, flinging his chuckle over his shoulder as he rode off in style.

It was fine with me to skip the crab feed. While swinging those Lions women around the dance floor was my only interaction with the opposite sex aside from club whores, I much preferred the humans on the dating site, Plugr.

I whipped by Taco Smell to get Tyrone's order, proud of myself for skipping the so-called vegetarian bean burrito. In addition to my pooper scooping chores, I was basically the main chef in the Jefferson's kitchen. I hadn't eaten much during my meth days in the holler. But plunging so suddenly into nutrition gave me a new zest for cooking, and it sure beat cleaning the men's toilet. Before I came around, PJ and Squee managed the kitchen, with uneven results. They were great at the manly art of grilling—peppering a piece of meat, tossing it on the grill, and staring at it.

But when Van Rossi came along, I introduced the subtle art of chilis, stews, and soups. I'd blow Tyrone away by going to the farmer's market to pick up green onions, beets, and brussels sprouts. Jackie Daytona even ate my sprouts once, after I'd drenched them in butter and bacon. Yeah, I was super into cooking. I'd starved for years when high on meth. I wanted to eat correctly along with my weight training, so I saved the butter and sugar for the others.

Crosley's Harley was in the alley, but there was no sound of him inside the darkened rooms. I fried up some parcooked sprouts and red onion with the ground beef, and ate maybe four ounces of it. After showering, I hit my little cave, turning on the laptop where the screen flickered against the Queen poster, bathing Freddie and Brian in an alien light. I took a hit of Magic Bus, the only substance I allowed myself to abuse anymore. I exhaled onto the screen, coating it with my hopes, terrors, and prayers for a new life.

Now I was Claude Berger, delivery driver from North Carolina.

I'd created this Finsta using some photos of a friend from the holler. With that as my base—plenty of photos of our old cat, bikes, and parties—I'd built this Plugr profile. I had a face, the face that gave me mortal horror to gaze upon, because I missed Claude with a passion. By using his face as my mask, I protected myself from exposure to Society's Bag while keeping Claude's memory alive. I even had a few shirtless photos to entice people.

DragonBoi had messaged me. His profile photo was one of those cheek-sucking duckfaces that made a person look botoxed. A masc for masc who was currently one mile away, I didn't dare risk a hookup. He liked my profile where I'd stated "Not seeking limp wrists, just someone to give me a limp." He liked staying in shape, but he was a fellow top, and I could just see us wrestling for power. The next message was from MascDoubtfire. He hid his location, but he'd sent me an unattractive dick pic. I can't explain what I didn't like about it. It was fine honestly. Just didn't do it for me. He said "Hey handsome," and was DDF and had a GSH — Drug and Disease-Free and Good Sense of Humor. He sarcastically "loved it when fats call themselves masc," which turned me off. I ghosted him, though we'd been chatting a couple weeks.

RaisedbyWolves was a fellow wolf currently hot to trot at a Henderson bar. He said "ew" to gaysians — gay Asians. I mean, I was as white as a nun's butt, but it still irritated me when I saw things like that. DapperDeveloper, an IT guy who lived in Vegas, suddenly needed an immediate hookup. "Best Western Bullhead City?" he suggested. "NSA, BB. BWC!" No strings attached, body builder with a big white cock. Still, I panicked.

I didn't look like Claude Berger. People might understand that I wanted to hide my doings from my boss. Still, it was really, really uncool on Plugr to basically fish someone, which I guess I was doing. I was the bad kind of fish — a catfish.

Society's Bag wasn't a club I wanted to spend my life with. I didn't know how long I could hold out with them, or how the finale would play out. When it did, I would have to leave Needles. I had contacts all over the US, though most were from my meth days. I could find somewhere to hide, bleach my hair, straighten it, get some ink.

Or, I could keep playing sex roulette on Plugr and eventually out myself. Society's Bag would smoke me, completely take me to the ground using one of their drawing and quartering methods, if they found out I had gay inclinations. I'd never have a chance to accomplish my mission. I'd have to slink back to the holler empty-handed, resuming my sorry life of cooking meth in a rancid trailer behind my mansion.

As Claude Berger, I could go to The Blue Oyster club in downtown Lake Havasu, the turf of Society's Bag's mortal enemies. I'd be safe there, humping meaty asses in the curtained back rooms. I could even wear a piece. Who would care if I covered up my hair? Claude and I had been to the only gay nightclub back in Laurinburg, the big city to us holler guys. We'd been too dazed by the otters in assless chaps, mannequins turned into cocktail tables, and handcuffed twinks in full David Bowie makeup to take any action. When someone groped my cock from behind, that was it. We blazed out of there in clouds of shame. It was not the scene for us yeehaws, us peckerwoods.

And then came StarGazer.

He was an absolute archangel from above. I expected him to break out a flaming torch while a halo shimmered above his head. I actually gasped, and allowed my pipe to flame out in the ashtray. StarGazer's glossy black locks were so tightly curled as to form a helmet around his skull. His exquisitely pointed nose made my prick harden, and his lips were absolutely cherubic, arched like Cupid's bow.

Oh. My. Saints.

He was like something God had just spit out.

He looked levelly at the camera as though he had nothing to hide, his long curls blanketing his shoulders. If his stats were true, he was a very tall slender man, thirty-seven, three hundred twenty miles away, and I had no reason to doubt him. His button-down shirt was open at the collar, revealing sparse chest hair. A fancy horn and turquoise pendant around his neck told me he was somewhat artsy, maybe into Native American stuff. His profession was just listed as "scientist."

I declare. I wanted this man of science to study *me.*

I was awestruck by his beauty. Why was such a stunning, accomplished man—for I instantly knew he was—wasting his time on Plugr? His profile gave me a clue.

Trying to come out with some dignity intact. New to this game.

So he was just now, at thirty-seven, coming out of the closet? *Well, I'll be, welcome to my fucking world.* His plea for kindness told me he might be a bottom, if he was even aware of his status.

I instantly clicked on the chat balloon. And my brain froze.

Oh God oh God. What did I normally say? *'Sup?* would not cut it with this man. *Damnation!* My mind had suddenly turned into a kid's dissection project splayed on the desk! I could not think.

I realized I was so in awe of StarGazer that I was intimidated by him. I could just tell from his face he possessed a higher intelligence than me. He was a man of letters. I hadn't even finished high school. My foster father was so vicious I wound up fleeing to the hills when I was sixteen.

Oh my saints! What the fuck did I just type? I sound like a typing instructor, a job interviewer! StarGazer would think I was some kind of moronic trailer park all-star, some hillbillious son of the soil. *Oh well. Then he'll know the truth.*

I couldn't take it back. My eyes were just fixed on the fucking screen, looking at my asinine words. *He's probably talking to someone else. I can log out right now and not think about it, for now. Who the fuck cares what StarGazer thinks, anyway? If it took him this long to come out, he's probably just bicurious and stands everyone up anyway. I'm sure his wife just walked into the room. He's in Nevada, it must be the middle of nowhere. What a fucking hick from the sticks. Oh wait, I am a hick from the sticks. God, he has lustrous hair. I wonder how it would feel against my face? He has nice long fingers. I wonder how hard he'd get if I nibbled on his earlobe –*

"'Sup?"

Crosley Shelvador's half-assed voice startled me so I jumped. It must've looked mighty suspicious how I gasped and swiveled my torso to face him, clutching my chair. Luckily, Crosley wasn't too swift on the uptake. With his thumbs hitched into his jean pockets, he ambled around my side, that permanent goon grin pasted on his face.

He wasn't a bad guy, really. He'd just picked the damndest moment to bust into my room.

I wasn't fast enough minimizing my screen. I just lucked out that Crosley didn't fully realize what he'd seen.

He guffawed. "Oh, man! Fags trying to get you to suck their dick? What kind of a scientist is that guy? Let me see again."

He stood so close to my chair his stupid crotch was in my face, and I would've done anything to stop that. I maximized StarGazer's profile, omitting my peckerwood messaging. Maybe Crosley's disgust would help stop me from committing this sin again. "Yeah, totally cruising me. Who knows what kind of scientist. Probably lying about it, anyway. I need to get a better antivirus app for this thing."

"Wow," Crosley breathed, looming over my shoulder. "He looks like Brian May in this Queen poster."

I seriously had not noticed that. Maybe that's why, subconsciously, I had fixed so heavily on StarGazer. "Yeah, whatever. Who knows who tries to scam you in the middle of the night." I *Xd* out of the screen this time, giving Crosley no more time to talk about fags.

CHAPTER TWO

Huntington Mountjoy

I was trying to remember how I got stuck in a Comfort Inn in Tonopah, Nevada.

It had all been so sudden, although the tension had lain there under the surface for a decade or more. Our oldest daughter was seventeen, so I'd been walking on eggshells for nearly twenty years.

"Are you attracted to men?" my wife had asked me one day in the elevator leaving the therapist's office.

My heart did that thing you often hear about, stopping cold. When it thudded to a start again, I managed to inhale a small breath. We had discussed nothing of this nature during the session. "Sometimes," I stumbled. "I mean, ah, I've wondered sometimes."

She looked straight ahead at the elevator door. "Wondered what? What it would be like?"

"Ah, um, yeah, I suppose."

The door opened then, so it devolved into one of those strained, uneasy silences. My hands gripped the steering wheel and Lauren sat in utter silence. I was stuck behind a fucker going thirty-five, enclosing me in my little Jaguar capsule of shame. I was married to a woman and living a lie. This reality had been slapping me in the face the past several years. We saw the therapist regarding our daily trials with the girls and arguments over how money should be spent. But this exact subject had never come up.

At last I couldn't stand it, and blurted, "If anything, maybe I'm bi."

Lauren was too quick to agree. "Bicurious!" Reality must've beaten her over the head, too, because she added, "But that's still not good enough, Hunt. We can't stay married."

"Why not? What about the kids?" I realized I'd just uttered one of the corniest, most useless sentences known to man.

Lauren chuckled. "Because you're always going to be wondering, Hunt! I don't want to sleep with a man who's imagining some other guy's . . . " She trailed off. We were both from North Carolina, the most homophobic state in the union. They proudly led the nation in anti-gay violence. It just wasn't discussed. It was probably a little better in Tonopah, where I worked for the Army at a missile range. At least at my job it was probably slightly more open-minded. Engineers and physicists tended to be.

We drove by the Clown Motel. That was one of the reasons Tonopah was listed in the Encyclopedia of Forlorn Places. No one in my family had been thrilled I'd dragged them there. My jobs took me to far-flung areas of the continent, never anywhere anyone wanted to actually be. I had let down my entire family. "Lauren, I'm not going to let this tiny . . . *proclivity* tear apart our family. You know how much you mean to me."

"But it's more like we're *friends*. Have been for years."

"Are you saying . . . " Now I drifted away. I didn't want confirmation of my unenergetic, slapshot lovemaking skills.

"No! You're wonderful in bed."

How good of a wife could Lauren possibly be?

She went on. "But I think it's best if we start sleeping separately. Kaitlyn is going off to school on the twentieth. You can take her room."

"But . . . " I didn't know where to start. "What are we going to tell Hannah?"

"We're telling her the second we get home, Hunt. You're attracted to men and that's that."

That wasn't just that, though. Hannah blubbered and cried, asked who else knew, and didn't talk to me for a month.

Kaitlyn, being a more mature sorority girl, tried to tell Hannah to get over it. Kaitlyn asked her sister, "Did he admit he's a drug dealer? Did he admit he's a rapist? A child molester? No? Then get over it."

When Lauren asked me directly, in private, if I had ever done anything with another man, I didn't lie then, either. I admitted that at Princeton I'd engaged in some man-on-man action, just a short while before meeting her. To my surprise, Lauren perked up at this. Demanded details. Randy had played Mozart, explained the meaning behind each song, and stroked the inside of my thigh. He'd prepared a candlelit chicken dinner for me, and then he speared his fingers through my hair. It didn't feel right. Yet it was so, so romantic.

"Do men kiss?" I'd asked.

"Want me to show you how?" Randy whispered, and kissed me.

I didn't struggle when he led me to the bed. Then I knew how helpless women feel when at the mercy of an assertive man. "I can't do this," I told Randy. "People are going to talk about us."

He never stopped smiling. "Well. Let's give them something to *really* talk about."

"And?" Lauren asked.

"And nothing. I panicked and ran from the room."

"Oh, Hunt . . . " Lauren said with pity. "You've been living a lie for so long. I'm just glad you gave me two daughters and a bunch of wonderful homes."

"I've stolen your joy," I admitted. "You're in love with a lie." Or . . . *was* she even still in love with me? Had I pulled the bait and switch on own wife? Now she was asking me to ghost her, as the kids would say.

"No," said Lauren. "You've saved your own life. I just have one question."

"Shoot."

"Why did you wait so long?"

That was easy. "Because I promised myself I'd never be a slut like my father. You know my mother kicked him out when I was ten." Lauren had never met him. We didn't even know where he was. "It was due to his cheating. So my mother turned against sex. You know she used to harass me about my weight."

"Well, yes. You *are* rather thin. Or *were.*"

"She used to worry about that. And the way it came out was quite . . . "

"Nasty." Lauren knew my mother.

"Right. She'd poke and prod at every perceived weakness. I was too skinny, a bad athlete, too effeminate. Each thing was a reflection on her, a disappointment, a shame. She'd say shit like 'You'll never be happy being a fag, Hunt. You'll have to move to Paris, have sex with everyone and get AIDS.' I endured her remarks for years. 'Your thigh is as big as my arm.' 'Don't put your hands on your hips.'"

Lauren finally laughed. "I've heard her talk about fudge packers, homos, fairies, poofs . . . I wondered what her obsession was."

"Well, it was me. That's when I threw myself into weightlifting—"

"—and steroids—"

Yes, she'd busted me not long ago on that. "—and steroids, and dating girls, convincing myself I was straight, going through the motions." I realized what I'd just said. *Going through the motions.* Like with Lauren.

She graciously ignored it. "Hunt, you're discriminating against yourself. If you can't accept yourself, how do you expect others to?"

In the end, we decided I'd get this shitty hotel room, which was actually closer to the missile range. With Kaitlyn at college, my remaining two girls could move back to Florida, Iowa, New Hampshire . . . any of the places we'd lived that they preferred.

But they were my life, my best friends. I couldn't see the logic in leaving them behind.

I spent even more time at work. I babysat the radar-based obstacle detection systems, coded, did research in molecular modeling and quantum interactions. Lately I'd been working with a subcontractor designing novel drug molecules to bind to protein targets. I was a jack of all trades, and even had a close friend, Dustin. We'd lunch together and stop for drinks on our way home at night. Was I in love with him? He was married, bless his heart. But over the past year we'd worked together, I'd come to rely on him, confided in him, and knew I'd tell him I thought I was gay. I had a craving, longing skin hunger for him.

I started out at the bar after work, telling him I'd moved into the motel. Of course he asked me why. I fiddled with the little straw I knew I shouldn't have accepted because of the turtles. No one should use those plastic disposable straws. I wound up fixating on the straw, and its sharp silhouette against my whiskey glass reminded me of a nebula I'd seen that day. It was choking with dusky dust clouds, a stunning Carolina Blue standing out sharply against glowing gas. It was a thing of beauty.

Dustin prompted me. "Troubles with Lauren?"

I'd never mentioned any troubles, because there weren't any, other than fighting over money and my apathy for having sex with her. I thought I'd been a pretty good actor. My standard script was mow lawn, ask kids about homework, and have sex with wife.

I finally straightened my spine in my chair. "Yeah. A pretty big trouble with her. The fact is Dustin . . . I'm gay."

He didn't respond right away, and this terrified me. I finally looked at him. A smile was starting at the edges of his mouth, but I couldn't tell if he was about to laugh or scoff.

Finally I had to prompt him. "Cumon, Dustin! *Say something!*"

He laughed. It wasn't unkind, just the sputtering of a pent-up amusement. With me, apparently. "Well, if that's not the biggest anticlimax of the fucking year, Hunt!"

I frowned. "What do you mean?"

He pressed his fingertips to his chest. "I sort of knew that."

I frowned even harder. "How?"

He shrugged, looked around at all the other straight patrons as if they could help him. "Hard to say, really. It's just . . . something. My cousin in San Francisco is gay. I just knew."

I banged my fist on the table. "Oh, if *that* isn't the most stereotypical thing on the planet! Gay in San Francisco. How about gay in Tonopah, Nevada with two teenaged children?"

Dustin sobered up. "*That* isn't so stereotypical. So you just now figured it out?"

"No," I admitted, back to sipping my drink, which now looked like a dying star. "I've known since adolescence. I've just been in denial."

Dustin asked the logical question. "What're you going to do about it? I can't think of anyone else at the test range who's homosexual, unless you count—"

I knew who he was thinking of. And it was grotesquely appalling. "Cameron Winkelvoss." I knew it, *I knew it.* Cameron Winkelvoss walked around with his belt up to his nipples sporting a Hitleresque moustache. He was perfect for the dull job of Chain of Custody Manager. "Do you know for a fact he's gay? I don't want to be looking on Grindr and seeing his fascist face."

"Not for a fact, because he never shows up at any of our social things. But can you picture him with a woman?"

"Neither one, frankly. He might be asexual. You know, nothing at all. So is *that* the sort of person y'all associate with being gay? Damnation!" I was falling back into my Scots-Irish Appalachian brogue because, I was upset. Weren't some homosexuals buff and hot? The ones I'd snuck a peek at on Grindr sure were. Unless they were using fake profile photos.

"Not at all!" Dustin raised his glass to me. "Look at you! You're one of the hottest guys at the range. The most banging hot astrophysicist, hands down."

I swelled with pride. "Go on." It wasn't like me to be arrogant, but I was in a vulnerable place. Someone had to be arrogant.

"Look at your fucking hair, man. You've just got lustrous, black, spilling, uh, locks. Looks like black snakes. You look like a fucking rock star. You're thin but muscular. Look like you should be some heavy metal guitarist."

I admitted, "I was in a band at Princeton. Played a guitar I made myself."

"Well, see what I mean? I feel like a no one next to you. I'm only a god damned QA test engineer. You're fucking *Doctor* Huntington Mountjoy, PhD. Those fucking gays will be crawling all over you!"

We proceeded to get fairly plastered, and I was glad Dustin was driving. In fact, the Comfort Inn was even more convenient for him on his way home to his own wife and two teenagers.

The last thing Dustin said to me was, "Don't worry about it, Hunt. You'll find someone really close to your heart. Maybe not Cameron Winkelvoss, but you'll find someone just as hot and intelligent as you."

I stumbled to my room, tossing my leather jacket on the upholstered armchair, and poured a fresh glass of whiskey without rocks. I needed this fortification lately to face the daily challenges, how radically my day-to-day life had changed, how much I missed Lauren and the girls.

But I had to investigate this.

I'd been messing around on Grindr and other gay dating apps. Plugr allowed you to write an entire bio, but when I read the other bios, I was quickly turned off with how many items they did *not* want. As usual, no one wanted Asians, but some guys really narrowed it down to, well, pretty much an actor named Ryan. Was I a Geek, Jock, or a Daddy? The only choices frustrated me. I'd been getting thinner since getting off steroids and I didn't want a workout buddy—who was anyone kidding?—so I chose Geek.

What was I into? How was I supposed to know until I tried it? Again, the narrow choices forced me to declare I was into Jocks, Muscles, and Geeks. I had put that I was into Friendships, Relationships, Dates, and Hookups. Y'all, I'm not apologizing for craving to check out that whole one night stand thing. Damnation, I wasn't even sure if I was a top or a bottom, a Dom or a sub! Was I just a bicurious married man?

Maybe Dustin would be the only romance I'd ever have.

"What do I do?" On all apps, I decided just to say "scientist." There was plenty of time to bore them to death later. I did mention I was coming out of the closet at this late date. That would explain my inexperience. I found out, to no one's surprise, that lots of men wanted to educate me. I was deluged with dick pics, to the point where I pondered deleting the part about the closet. I discovered that a headless dick pic floating in the atmosphere was not attractive. A few times, when they included their alleged torso and head, I became turned on enough to jack myself.

It was working. I was definitely gay.

Even then, they had to be a certain *type* that was difficult to describe. As a strong-nosed man myself, I liked that. I found myself prejudiced against anyone who resembled a baseball-capped, white supremacist ghettobilly. Biased against the exact place I'd grown up. It's really hard to describe how a man like this looked. A shady cast to his eyes, as though he was avoiding a key element of his own personality. I *owned* being a hill person, having yanked myself up from the sludge.

But I didn't want anyone who still lived there. He would not be sensitive to my plight.

So I guess I looked for city men. I avoided the Village People guys with the assless chaps, shiny vinyl caps, and porn 'staches, as I found they were called. Yet the Sam Elliott look made me hard. Distilling everything I desired was a process. Ultimately, I needed someone who could relate to my anxieties. Leaving my wife and children was not a simple procedure, and they'd still be in my world. Did this mean I wanted a man IRL, in real life? I would ghost anyone who didn't respond, then sent me musical recommendations a week later.

I wanted someone who knew himself better than I did. A photo could be slightly off, could literally show a man in the wrong light, add or delete a bump in his nose, make his arms look too short. Or an absolutely stunning man could quickly reveal himself to be an utter jethro.

I was about to shut it down and shower for the night. Tomorrow was another twelve-hour day writing code and being at the telescope—I'd waited months for my turn at that thing. Light from stars had travelled millions of years to reach me, so I needed to witness it.

Then came SoulWrestler.

His simple "How are you?" flung my missile range a trillion miles away.

I was entranced with his main profile photo. A masculine body builder, he was displaying a colossal chinook salmon he'd caught. Although he wore shades, his absolutely sparkling smile told me he was undamaged enough to be thrilled with a fish. A thirty-two-year-old delivery driver down in Bullhead City, he was more geographically desirable than most of these seekers. In another photo, he posed, again shirtless, against a backdrop of apricot and coral autumn trees. In *some* hills, but not *of* the hills.

His tightly cropped curly hair was starting to grey, and I liked that. I was no butt pirate, no lover of twinks. Although SoulWrestler's chest seemed hairless, he may have waxed it for weightlifting—or photo op—purposes.

He'd said "how are you?" an hour ago and that was all, yet I was swept away. I could just tell he was *sincere*, and that affected me. Well enough to finally respond,

"I just told my best friend I'm gay."

I sent it, and was pondering whether to add another remark when my cell rang.

It was a callback from Fremont Zuckerman in Lake Havasu. Fremont was a mining geologist I'd met on another job. Now he was saving Native Americans from uranium poisoning on some rez.

And he was gay.

Fremont had never outright *said* that to me. He just mentioned he was shacking up with a priest whom he called his "soul mate." He'd also, weirdly, joined this motorcycle gang, a rough group who seemed to be outlaws. I only knew that from googling The Bent Zealots MC. An article mentioned a high-speed police chase, a biker leading them on a 25 mile escapade through a river and a desert. The biker was finally stopped by an organ pipe cactus. The guy, a Havelock Singer, told them his wife was in labor. But in the middle of the desert? Another article mentioned a rumble at a local Bed Bath and Beyond. Someone was shot in the linen section, and the article made a point of mentioning that a yogurt making machine was used to knock a guy unconscious. Again, a Bent Zealot member named Brick Mantooth was a culprit in this.

I could never imagine Fremont as a proponent of this sort of idiocy. Yet he'd texted me photos of himself wearing a "cut," a leather vest decorated with biker insignia patches, standing next to this hot priest. Man, was the priest hot. Long, shiny, mocha hair around his shoulders, with large expressive hands folded in front of his crotch. Fremont had scored. But I had never dared share in his joy.

Now we'd been talking about maybe getting together in Lake Havasu, if I ever got more than one day off at a time.

"Fremont, my man."

"Hey, Dr. Mountjoy." He always said this somewhat ironically, bless his heart. Since we were good friends, he didn't need to address me like that. But my ego liked it. "Seen any dark matter lately?"

"I actually have," I admitted. "Part of my job is to make sure space is clear of space junk for the missiles."

"Yeah." Fremont sighed. He was basically a tree-hugging hippie at heart, as was I. "There's a lot of that flying around lately. Hey, listen. Noel wants to meet you. I want you to meet him. Come down to Havasu. Have dinner."

"Man, I'd love that," I admitted. "I've been staying at this fucking Comfort Inn, just a dismal hole in the wall. I'd love to blow the dust from my soul." I thought of SoulWrestler, driving an Amazon truck in suburbia or whatever he did, shirtless. Bullhead City wasn't far off my route to Lake Havasu. I could risk having some coffee or whatever.

"Why are you at a Comfort Inn?"

"Oh, ah, it's closer to the missile range," I lied. Fremont wouldn't look it up. "We're working ten tens. I can break loose the twentieth."

"Perfect," said Fremont. "We have to be in Lake Havasu for a fish fry. You want to meet us there?"

I didn't know what was so important about a fish fry, but I said sure. When Fremont gave me the address at some suburban area in the mountains above the lake, he said, "This is Lock Singer's house. He's the Veep of our club."

Lock Singer. The guy leading the cops on a wild goose chase to find a giant cactus. "Sure," I found myself saying. "I'm up for an adventure."

Fremont's tone changed then. "I have to tell you something, though. This might switch your mind."

I chuckled. "Oh, not much would surprise me right now."

"Well, the fact of the matter is . . . we're gay. All of us — or almost all of us. We're a bent outlaw biker club. There. I said it. Now, I know you're a happily married, straight, PhD graduate of Princeton. If this makes you feel uncomfortable, we can just meet at a diner —"

"No!" I raced to say. "Not at all!" Was I too eager?

Fremont sounded surprised. "Well, wow. I wasn't expecting this. Sounds great, Hunt. You're really taking it in stride. You know I was a happily married man too—"

"Kelly." Our wives had actually met, and had done a few things together. "Yes, yes. You came out? With the priest?"

"Yes! He still has his chapel, St. John's of the Desert, with a big Navajo contingent. No one seems to mind, though it disappointed a lot of the ladies."

"I'll bet. No, it doesn't bother me. Doesn't bother me at all. I'll see you at the fish fry the twenty-first." I was going to sleep over somewhere, wasn't sure yet. Maybe somewhere in Bullhead City.

We hung up, and I looked at my unanswered response to SoulWrestler. He was still online, but hadn't reacted to my revelation to my best friend. I'd just told my best friend I was bent, and Fremont had just told me. Men were speaking their honest, truthful selves all over the world.

Now I, a newly out man, would be attending an all-male biker fish fry. It would be a revelation. Maybe I'd meet the infamous Brick Mantooth. And Twinkletoes—real name Arthur Bukowski—another Bent Zealot that journalists claimed had laid down and "planked" in the middle of a downtown street pothole just to prevent a rival bike club from rolling through. They rolled anyway, one of them right over Twinkletoes' back.

But I still hadn't told Fremont I was gay.

CHAPTER THREE

Van Rossi

The bar area of Jefferson's always reeked of piss, beer, and puke.

We let everyone smoke inside. The bartender Pinky was a rough and tough woman who slid me a beer with hands like steaks, her vinyl-rimmed cap reflecting green fluorescent lighting from above. Doobie Brothers emanating from tinny speakers throbbed in my skull. Was it my imagination, or was Crosley Shelvador giving me a knowing look?

Oh, he was giving the evil eye to some outsider guy. Anyone who wanted could come into our bar. After all, it was on a public street, the dismal, dusty, barren old Route 66. The outsider looked like someone who'd climbed out of a dumpster. His jiggling belly boasted a swastika, his handlebar 'stache dripping with gristle.

Worse, he was eyeballing Tyrone Shoelace's old lady. I forget her name now, but she was actually a pretty brunette missing that vacant, dead look of a tweaker. I grabbed a pool stick and backed away from the intruder. *Where's Tyrone?* Ah, right on cue, Tyrone waddled over and bashed the interloper in the skull with his fist. The guy swished sideways off his stool as if blown by a hurricane.

And that was it. At least, for the interior of the bar. The guy stood, held his head, glared at Tyrone and left the bar. However, on his way down Route 66 he knocked over several bikes—intentionally or not, I don't know. I was one of the members out front jotting down the guy's license number. I had a way of running licenses without bothering the DMV.

Tyrone swatted me. "Find out where he lives."

"You got it, sir."

That guy's truck was history. Society's Bag would kick in the fenders, take baseball bats and hammers to the windows, and steal everything worthwhile from the engine. We'd stomp the guy into nuggets. No involvement of cops, no courtrooms, no nothing. His story would prevent anyone further from entering Jefferson's with an eye toward any woman's boobs.

Back inside the sweaty cave, Pinky had shut the music off and men huddled over beers, discussing their next run. Jackie Daytona approached me, hand out. This time he asked for eight Norco.

"Eight?" queried Crosley. "Man, you're really getting addicted to that shit."

Normally that would be a statement worthy of at least a facial slapdown. Society's Bag was just one mean, angry club. But tonight, Jackie was in a mellow mood, at least toward his club members.

He gulped four pills with a slug of beer and said, "I'm leery of getting into opioids. Wouldn't want to turn into a *real* addict. Besides, doctors look at you like you're some 'drug-seeking individual.' I guess I could go to those off-market places, the Silk Road, for some off-brand fentanyl."

I said, "You don't want fentanyl. Look what happened to Prince." No one seemed to know who Prince was. Truthfully, I just didn't want to picture a snarling, vicious Jackie Daytona on fentanyl. "Once you get into that, you keep needing more and more. No, you need to get some imaging done, Jackie. Find out exactly what's going on in your back."

"I have no fucking insurance," Jackie reminded me. "An MRI would cost seven thousand dollars."

I tossed my head. "We make that. Sell some iron."

Jackie tossed his head. "I wouldn't take that from the club. Besides, the fucking Chinese who make all these drugs are squeezing us. Prices are just going up and up, and our fucking postal service is getting slower and slower. FDA keeps raising drug prices. Something needs to be done to squeeze the Chinese."

This was when Crosley blurted out, "Van knows a scientist!"

"*What*?" I mouthed. I didn't want to believe what he was referring to. I had hoped that whole incident a few days ago was a nightmare. I had not logged back into Plugr since then.

Jackie said the word aloud. "*What*? You mean, like, someone who can make drugs for us?"

Crosley just kept on blarting. "Well, his gay screen name was StarGazer. So maybe he can control a satellite to spy on the Chinese."

I waved a disgusted arm. "Oh, what in the fucking name of—"

Jackie waved back at me. "Van, who you holding out on? And what you talkin' about, Crosley? What 'gay screen name'?"

Crosley's yaw was wide open, but I yelled louder than him. "Some gay guy was catfishing me, or at least the virus looked that way. I completely shut down my computer, man."

Crosley simultaneously yammered. "Yeah, I guess some fag thought Van's dating profile looked hot. If I was an ass bandit I probably would, too."

Jackie graced me with a rare smile. He looked like some Victorian doorman with his piled-up ash blond hair, his relative absence of ink. "Dating profile? What's wrong with our sweetbutts?"

I tried not to look around at the skanky tweakers who inhabited our den, jointless waifs draped over Society's Bag members. "Nothing at all, man. But I'm not supposed to blow a hole through anyone, right?"

"True, true," Jackie acknowledged. I had no time to date, theoretically. All my time was supposed to be dedicated to the club. "Then what're you doing with a dating profile?"

I dared to backhand Crosley on the chest. I could because he was the newest, and dopiest, member. "I don't *have* one! All Crosley saw was a photo of this guy catfishing me."

"Catfishing?" To my chagrin, Tyrone now inserted himself into the small crowd gathered around me. PJ and Squee were there, chuckling at all the gay references. I swear. "That's hilarious. You should catfish him back, just to see what he says."

"Yeah, yeah!" echoed Squee. "See what he says!" What a doofus.

"Yeah, yeah!" declared Gangbang Greg. "See if he wants to suck your dick."

What was their problem? Why the sudden interest in whether another guy wanted to suck my dick?

Thankfully, Tyrone yelled, "Stow it!" And the outlaws did.

But Jackie kept on. "This catfisher's a scientist. I want to see if Van the Man here can get him to help us. Making cheap painkillers. I don't trust One Nut Nick. His recent proposal to make morphine reeked like —"

"Sulfuric acid," I injected.

Jackie looked taken aback. I kept trying to tell them I used to make meth, but they didn't seem to believe me. Besides, I highly doubted StarGazer was that sort of scientist. But as a Prospect, I had to play along.

Jackie continued, less confidently. "I didn't trust his proposal. I want to get someone with an in with the Chinese. Import it directly. Or make it in a decent lab. Think what a great new gig that'd be for us."

Tyrone shrugged. "Sure, worth a try. Van, you pal around with this scientist. That's your new order."

Crosley said, "Just think if this guy has a telescope! We could spy on the Chinese!"

Incredibly, Tyrone seemed to consider that idea. "Sure, why not? Maybe he's closeted. We could blackmail him into letting us use his telescope."

I tried not to scoff out loud. "Sir, respectfully, we don't even know what kind of scientist this guy is. He could be a gas station owner. He could be lying, like most of these catfishers. He could be a fucking gym owner."

"Or a gym *goer*," Crosley noted.

Tyrone stuck a forefinger into my chest. "Yeah, you go catfish this guy right back. Pretend to be a poof. See what you can blackmail him into."

"All right, sure," I said, just to get them to shut the fuck up. At this point, I almost felt protective of "my" StarGazer. How dare these fucking filthy outlaws infringe on StarGazer's pristine, thoughtful, and sensitive state? He did claim to be a Geek, seeming to have no awareness that he was definitely a wolf too. Wolves were lean, muscular, and only semi-hairy—yet sexually aggressive. Could I handle another Dom? I did like the power struggle that could ensue between two assertive Doms. "Let me make these guys their pizza."

I made excuses all evening, and I definitely had enough excuses to avoid going to my computer. I even lied that StarGazer was only online late at night. By the time I'd rolled out, topped, and baked the pizza, washed dozens of beer mugs at least twice, and replaced the toilet paper in the bathroom, everyone was gone. The last person to leave was Pinky, and she said some mighty odd stuff to me.

"Don't let them get you down."

"About what?"

She seemed to keep winking at me, like we were both in on some joke. "You know. The gay-bashing. There's nothing wrong with liking the same sex."

I was completely taken aback. "Bless your heart," was all I could think to say. I'd never stopped to consider that Pinky was a lesbian. Now it was pretty damned obvious. She wore suspenders over her sturdy, distended stomach. Her impish face was cute, like a young child. A non-filter cigarette hung from her lower lip.

Her voice was flat, matter-of-fact. "I know you can't tell those guys to go to hell, but you might consider doing it when you get fully patched. Just remember. These aren't civilized people. These are outlaws."

I lifted my chin. "I'm used to it. I'm from the hollers of North Carolina."

She nodded in assent. "I figured it. So you know how unpopular ball-licking can be. My advice to you is to keep it on the down low."

"Keep *what* on the down low? You just heard. Tyrone *tasked* me with catfishing this, uh, this scientist."

Pinky firmed her jaw. "You're gay, Van. Other queers can tell. Don't deny it. Is it obvious you're sitting there thinking about some goddamn dick-licking, nipple-ring-twanging, ass-slapping cock? Yes. Yes it is, to me. Maybe not to these local yokels. So play things close to the vest."

Without admitting anything I said, "Well, I intend to. Thanks for the advice, Pinky. Now if you'll excuse me."

"I know. You need to shower. Especially after being rained on by all this B.O. and spit all day." She put her cigarette out in an ashtray instead of on the floor like some did. I was the one who had to wash the floor.

"Well, yes, shower. And I need to go catfish some fag."

Pinky frowned. "Don't use that word. Especially not if you're one." And she stomped out the front door, to whatever apartment hovel she inhabited with other suspendered ladies.

I did shower. Pinky was right—I always felt creepy-crawly after a day with those men, even if on an outdoor run. My cock was up like a hammer at the idea of catfishing StarGazer. I mean, I knew it was morally wrong to lure some guy into meeting, under false pretenses. But I was *already* doing that. I was *already* pretending to be Claude Berger. How much worse if I asked him to make us painkillers?

I'd have to do the fishing first, though. I leaned against the shower enclosure, my eyes sliding shut, my hand slipping to my soapy prick. I told myself I wasn't intentionally jacking myself thinking of StarGazer's cascading curls, his heroic, aquiline nose. My palm cupped my full balls as I languidly pumped my cock, having no intention in the world of coming, unless it was by accident. Those sudden ones sometimes took me by storm. But I remained in control, as though playing a slow tease game of orgasm denial with myself. With regret I rinsed off, but admired my hard-on in the mirror after I got out.

Man, that would make a nice selfie. I'd never sent a dick pic to anyone, but I was maybe about to start.

I peeked into Crosley's room to make sure he was asleep. He was. He had a cot and sleeping bag like I did, and one of those folding racks where you drape your wet clothes. His laptop was open, so I tiptoed over to see if there was any blackmail evidence I could use against him in the future, to shut him up. I was hoping for something gay, but it was just a message to his mother.

A pretty nice Saturday. I'm going to Home Depot to get some window replacements for our clubhouse. The last ones were bashed out in some kind of accident. Do you like the double paned?

Wow. If that wasn't blackmail material, I didn't know what was.

Mom! Can I get your berry pie recipe? What're you doing? You never talk to me anymore.

Wow. Just *wow.* He seriously wrote this shit to her? I had no idea where my mother was. She had abandoned me into foster care when I was ten, too strung out to get a job and support a child.

Sighing louder now, as though unafraid of being caught, I went back to my room. When I sat in my chair, my cock flopped around at half-mast, so I secured it with my palm. I looked at my profile on Plugr. I scrolled through Claude Berger's photos to ensure they were enticing enough. I was Masc, that was for fucking sure, DDF—aside from weed, which I now fired up in a bowl— and Discreet on the DL. Instead of listing that I was into hookups or relationships, I just said I had No Agenda. NSA, no strings attached. I was 420 Friendly, y'all.

Probably due to his recent coming-out, StarGazer was "straight-acting." That was nice. Who wanted someone flitting around as if wearing ballet shoes? There was one amazing photo of him — if indeed it was him — with a silk shirt unbuttoned to *here*, his sterling turquoise pendant gleaming richly. A profile shot, it really showed off that aquiline schnozz to great advantage. The only way I could describe his teeth was pearly white. They were such adorable little snowy nubs, not crooked or rotten every whichway like in the holler.

With an inhalation and a squeeze of my cock, I opened the message box.

STARGAZER: I just told my best friend I'm gay

Why, the poor thrillbilly sounded downright depressed. Then it struck me. *I should be empathetic. Not one of my strong suits.* Growing up viewing every new introduction as a potential enemy out to do you harm, it was a rare occasion when I got to know someone who *didn't* shit on my campfire after stabbing me in the back. That was the way of the holler.

I rubbed my chin as I thought. *Empathy, empathy.* Many times my index finger started for the keyboard, and many times I drew it back. I wasn't even thinking of my cock now.

Then it struck me all at once. I'd been in his exact shoes not long ago. There was no way in hell I could exit the closet in Hank's Hot Springs, North Carolina. In a way it was a good thing I came here, because when I was done avenging Claude Berger I could actually find a town, find a job to do with welding, and what do you know, actually *be* gay.

StarGazer seemed to be looking for The One.

Did I care about any of that? Was I willing to put my entire life on the line for some man who might stomp my soul intro smithereens? Damnation, this man was so beautiful I might even risk my whole plan involving Tyrone Shoe—

What in damnation was I thinking? Tyrone was my nemesis, a rabid pig direct from hell, and I could let nothing stand in my way of—

Oh my saints. What in the name of Thomas Alva Edison had I just typed? I frantically looked for the "delete" icon, but once I found it, I couldn't bring myself to hit it. Besides, StarGazer would know that I'd deleted something. In a panic, I tore down the hallway to the kitchen and whisked a Pabst Blue Ribbon from the fridge. I'd drunk enough of that shit in the holler to fill the Dead Sea. I'd thought I was done with it, but now I wanted one more than ever.

I stood in the hallway gulping it, panting like a motherfucker. Here I was, plotting to ice the Prez of an MC, and I couldn't even DM with another man. Had I really been on my solo mission for that damned long? Claude had been murdered a year and a half ago. What kind of a lame local yokel was I? I consciously tried to slow my breathing, to "breathe deep" as yoga teachers told women.

Dreading what, if anything, I'd see when I got back to my room, I headed there like I was trudging through a blizzard. Plunking my ass on the chair and the beer on the desk, I forced my eyes open.

Oh my saints. I was too stunned to even gulp the beer.

I slapped my own forehead. He was waiting for me to reply.

I could picture his intelligent chocolate brown eyes looking at the screen, waiting for me. How had StarGazer raised himself from the holler to become a scientist? I couldn't imagine this angelic man sleeping in a decrepit, rotting shack, an old Barcalounger residing on his front lawn. Would he have a starving dog chained up there too?

So I typed:

CLAUDE: *You from the holler too?*

STARGAZER: *Yes, extremely so. My three siblings and I all slept in the attic. Luckily the mountains were a godsend. I spent most of my time outdoors.*

He said "and I"! He has "siblings"! Damnation, this scientist was way too hifalutin for me. But I hadn't talked about North Carolina to anyone in months. So I typed on.

CLAUDE: *I started out in Laurinburg, but wound up in the backwoods holler near Hank's Hot Springs. So great to meet another ghettobilly, especially on Plugr.*

I just whaled on the *send* icon, that's how carried away I was getting. As I waited for StarGazer's reply with bated breath, I realized *I'm in love with this guy.* I wanted to know more, more, more!

But I'm supposed to be catfishing him.

Massachusetts, that explained something. Probably Princeton. I reckoned catfishing didn't necessarily mean making up a completely new persona, at least not my history. It'd be easier to remember if I kept to the facts, so I admitted to him:

I didn't want to discuss any sort of meth-making, so I fell back on the Claude Berger resumé:

I waited eagerly for Star's response. *Murderation, I'm already calling him Star.* I wanted so badly to ask for a shirtless pic. But now we'd established a friendly dialogue, it would feel sort of awkward to segue into horny talk like that.

Yet I was. Horny.

I had his four profile pics up — the flaming archangel, him playing a guitar and looking randy, him in the sun wearing a rather artsy jacket with symbols all over it, and yeah, Star himself leaning sideways next to some kind of telescope, as if he were nude and the machine was a girl.

Only we didn't care about girls.

My heart thudded. *Meeting? No Agenda? Already?* This had not been that difficult!

In my excitement, I typed:

CLAUDE: That would be great. Shirtless pic?

Oh, Lord, what a ghettobilly! I was just proving my whole point about what a hilliterate I was! Yet I didn't erase it. I needed to reel him in, after all. And to do that, we needed to connect on a sexual level, not just a holler one.

I waited, palming my hard-on. I allowed my thumb to drift over the bulging head, imagining I even felt it throb beneath my loving hand. I wanted this beautiful man's face between my thighs.

I waited some more, considering taking my cock out and jacking myself to those saintly photos. That aristocratic nose nuzzling around my pubic bone, the pointed tongue darting out to lick the root of my prick, his hot breath against my ballsac, all this drew me higher, higher. I didn't even need to smoke the weed or drink the beer to vividly picture this man's tongue thrusting around my balls. I must've gotten carried away, because when I next looked back at the screen, nothing had moved.

Nothing.

I'd scared him off with the shirtless request.

Now I really pounded myself in the forehead with my palm. *What a fucking jethro!* I started fixing to orgasm and I forgot to entice my number one target!

I ran to the kitchen to grab another PBR. With each gulp I prayed that StarGazer was typing. *Type, man, type! Oh, how could I be so moronic? He wanted to meet. I didn't need a fucking shirtless pic. I'd see him in the flesh. Then I could fondle his crotch.*

Fuck! I ran back down the hallway, knowing if I met up with Crosley stumbling to the bathroom I'd sock him in the throat. I wanted desperately to see my computer screen, yet I never wanted to see it again.

Nothing.

StarGazer had ghosted me over a shirtless pic.

CHAPTER FOUR

Hunt

SoulWrestler was coming clean about himself.

I knew this, because no one would admit to living in Hank's Hot Springs. It was a dismal hole, people walking around with hollow eyes like *Walking Dead* actors. Meth mouth added years, if not decades, to their age. Guys who could find time to have eight children, but too lazy to support them. "Mountain Dew Mouth" gave youngsters the look of oldsters. Because amphetamines hindered your appetite, people had shrunken, wasted muscles, their elbows and knees protruding.

SoulWrestler had come west. His photos and profile both attested to his workout regime. And who knew, maybe he'd never been a meth head. I was just assuming. If he drove a delivery truck he'd probably be drug tested once in awhile, like we were at the airfield. No. This guy was worth taking a little risk for.

So I typed:

> STARGAZER: *We have so much in common, SoulWrestler.*
> *We should meet. NA.*

No agenda. My heart skittered around, looking at those words on the screen. I'd never typed them to anyone.

And I waited. And waited.

Was this guy the slowest typist in the world? I guessed a mountaineer wouldn't have much opportunity to utilize a keyboard—especially not like an astrophysicist. I didn't want to be hoity-toity, but there *were* radical differences between us. Still, did a lover need to satisfy *all* of your needs? Lauren, although a marketing director, never read books at home. She watched TV. I read books in my study. Did that make us incompatible? I loved to fish, to camp, to hunt. She'd prefer, well, maybe wine tasting. So we had a lot of separate interests. It had never created any palpable irritations for us.

I blinked. The light in this Comfort Inn was horrible, fluorescent. It gave me a sort of photosensitive epilepsy where my vision shuddered and fluttered. Almost like a brain zap where you had to shake your head, remember where you were. My heart beat off-kilter, not once but twice. I wiped sweat from my forehead with the back of my hand.

Then a pain gripped me, right at the base of my trachea. Did I have heartburn? That happened sometimes when I accidentally got a soda with fake sugar, sucralose or some garbage. My idiot onscreen words inviting SoulWrestler into my life suddenly gave me anxiety. *Who am I fucking kidding? I had sex with* one *man,* one *time.* I was as ignorant as an Asian stumbling into Plugr for the first time. Though I'd said I had no agenda, I really had one.

I wanted a lover. A long-term relationship.

Sure, it'd be great to gulp a nice healthy meaty prick again. It would be great to be fucked up the ass by some top, a built masc guy who loved lording it over me. Or would Randy at Princeton be the only romance I'd ever have? My jaw, the back of my neck seized up then, like an elephant sat down on my chest, and I had to fling my torso back in the chair.

This was no heartburn. This was a heart attack.

I grabbed my phone off the desk and thumbed Dustin's number. We'd had a strange, stiff relationship since I'd come out to him. We hadn't had drinks, even though he knew I was living in a fucking Comfort Inn. We were stuck working on algorithms together at work sometimes, but we just did that like we were your average coworkers, not the best friends I'd imagined we were.

"Hello?"

"Dustin."

"Hunt." He sounded relieved.

"I'm having a heart attack."

"What? Well call fucking 911! No, *I* will! Are you at the hotel?"

I submitted to Dustin's management. The EMTs came before Dustin got there. By that time, I think I was on the floor writhing. A woman did chest compressions, and soon a guy came in to jolt me with the defibrillators. I was especially angry when he tore off the pendant I always wore around my neck, a bear's claw encased in silver and turquoise. A cartoonish automated voice seemed to come from the machine, telling him to *shock me now!*

I tell you, my mind was yonder somewhere out in space by the time this happened, although logically it felt like I was kicked by a kangaroo in the chest. I knew they were zapping me because my body jerked, crying out for my mind to return. People milled and muttered around me. But my soul was somewhere out past Betelgeuse.

I declare, I was talking to some sort of spirit guides. We floated airlessly, the earth a speck just like all the other billion stars. We spoke this lingo that was too highly intelligent for my human brain. We discussed lofty matters I couldn't remember later. I've strived for years to recall even a topic, all of which seemed worthy of Einstein, but it was like my higher power didn't want me to remember. It was too much for a simple human to fathom. Our brains would explode if we knew all this stuff.

I came back to Earth briefly in the parking lot, Dustin running at my gurney's side. I'd never seen him so panicked, not even when one of his kids got hit in the head with a baseball. *He's really my friend.*

"Hang in there, buddy. Just hang tight. Stay with us. Don't go anywhere. Nothing would be the same without you."

I questioned every dubious step I'd taken. What if my mother had loved me the way I'd been, a skinny youth as tall as a steeple? What if I had not married Lauren? Hannah and

Kaitlyn would never have existed. But if I'd never moved to Nevada I wouldn't have run into Dustin . . . and SoulWrestler.

An endless night of beeping monitors and wires ensued. They gave me some horse tranquilizer that had me floating away like I swung in a hammock, vaguely dizzy yet light as a particle. The spirit guides didn't return, and I dreamed of SoulWrestler.

Looking about as flat and two-dimensional as his profile photo, and even gripping the same flat giant striper he'd just caught, he tormented me with his sleazery. "I fucked this guy last night," he taunted, "and he was better than you'll ever be. Hot. You're not hot, and you'll never be. Look how you put your hands on your hips! You're too skinny. You're a fairy, a fag. I'm masc! I'm 2Masc4U!"

I had a fucked morning, grunting at the nurses who came to check on me. Dustin finally entered with some sort of packaged Dingdongs in his hand. He looked so surprised that my eyes were open, he practically dropped the donuts and strode to grab a chair by my bed.

"Hunt! Are you okay? Fuck, you had me so scared for awhile there!"

I sighed. The action hurt my ribcage, as though my heart was bruised. I found I was constantly sighing, that I had a shallow lung capacity, and fatigue would follow me for weeks. "Yeah. I'm fine. But I need to make some fucking changes."

"Oh *yeah*, for sure! The doctor said your blood pressure is one-fifty over ninety-three. Your total cholesterol is two-forty and the bad LDL is one-ninety! It's got to be all that junk we eat." He glanced at the delinquent Dingdongs.

It actually hadn't occurred to me it was our lousy roach coach diet making me sick, because I continued to work out at the airfield gym. Since getting off steroids, I'd gone from an eight-pack to a four-pack. "No, I wasn't thinking of Pringles and Snickers." I tried to wipe my face with my palm, but my arm was stuck to some wire. "I know I told you I was gay. Now I don't know. I'm just confused."

"No doubt," Dustin said with sympathy.

"I need to take some time off from the missile range."

"For sure! The doctors will *force* you to, at the very least. He said you'll have to go to cardiac rehab."

I didn't care about that. "No, I was talking about moving. I can't live in a fucking hotel anymore. Maybe get some Airbnb in Lake Havasu. Go fishing."

Dustin sighed as though a huge weight had been lifted off him. "That's the best, bro! Forget all this homosexual stuff. Take Lauren with you to Lake Havasu."

What? That wasn't what I was thinking at all. I was more like hoping that Fremont and Father Noel could come and talk some sense into me, remind me of all the things I'd always done that were gay as hell. I *wanted* to be gay, I really did. Lauren had paved the way by setting me free. But I was still having deep doubts about my path. "No, no, I really *want* to explore 'this homosexual stuff,' as you call it."

Dustin frowned. "You *do*? Because man, I was going to tell you, ah . . . I don't think I can hang out with a homosexual guy. Really, Hunt. It just creeps me out too heavily to picture a friend of mine doing that. I was talking to Leslie about it."

"You told Leslie?"

He laughed nervously. "Well, why not? She *is* my wife. Speaking of, I called Lauren, of course. It'll take awhile for her to get here because she took Hannah up to Lake Powell. A vacation, you know, after you dropped that bomb on them."

I tried to sit up. It wasn't just that I was encased in wires — I was also weak as hell. "Lake Powell? What the fuck? No one told me. So wait. You're not going to hang out with me anymore? No drinks after work? No shooting range?"

"I'm sorry, man. I thought long and hard about it." Then he must've realized he'd said something gay-centric, for he blushed and coughed. "It's just not in my wheelhouse. I wish you the best of luck, of course. I'm going to wait here until your other friend comes."

"No, don't bother." If I was going to sink into a deep funk, which I was bound to do, I didn't want Dustin hanging around, his judgmental face making everything ten times worse. I was beyond fed up with being unloved because of who I was. I rolled away from Dustin like a sullen baby. "Just go."

"I'm really sorry, Hunt. I just thought a lot about it. It makes me too uncomfortable."

I let him off the hook. "Don't worry. I'm going to get that a lot. Might as well get used to it now."

I was amazed when I heard the door shut. He fucking walked away, just like that! Since when in today's modern fucking world was being gay such a scarlet letter? I steamed myself so thoroughly, huffing through my nostrils, that my heartrate monitor started beeping, sending a nurse in to check on me. *A male nurse.*

I thought about what Dustin had said, "until your other friend comes." *Too bad I can't text him, ask him what he meant.* This dilemma was solved within the hour when Fremont came in my door.

I hadn't seen him in so long. And now he was seeing me, weak and connected to machines. Fremont was even heartier and buffer than before, wafting the fresh scent of the outdoors. I saw him through the morphine haze, dripping into my arm.

"Fremont." I tried to sit up, but he held out a palm, telling me to stay. He sat in the same chair Dustin had just vacated, and my blurry brain was conflating the two. My beeping heart rate soared again. I stopped struggling. "I heard Dustin called you."

His voice was smooth and soothing, like a news announcer. He threaded his fingers together as he leaned forward, just the proper amount of concern in his voice. "Yeah, yeah. He couldn't get ahold of Lauren. I figured we already had the fish fry plans, it's no big deal for me to ride up here."

"Riding" reminded me Fremont was now in a biker club. I squinted my eyes to see the patches on his leather cut. I chuckled. "The Bent Zealots. I can't believe it. You were always such a hippie."

Fremont grinned, one-sided. "I know. The two aren't really incompatible though. Us bikers do a lot of hippie things. Like go to the farmer's market. Burning Man, music fests."

"Except you kill people at music fests." What was I thinking? Where did I get that idea? The Rolling Stones at Altamont? Yet I heard it come from my mouth. Was I some kind of prejudiced, anti-biker guy?

Fremont reached out and touched my cheek. There it was, that skin hunger I'd increasingly felt the past many months. I craved to be touched, and by another man. Endorphins shot through me like a vaccination, infusing all my cells. I never wanted him to stop, and my hand reached up to hold his still.

"You could've died, man," Fremont said softly. "What the fuck were you thinking?"

Squeezing my eyes shut, I formed some words. "I was talking to another gay man on the computer. The stress just became overwhelming. I don't know if I can navigate this coming out business."

Fremont's hand stilled. "What? What are you talking about?"

I had to say it. "I think I'm gay too, man."

I don't know how long we remained stock-still. Were we even breathing? The only thing that attested to time moving along was the monitor beep, the flickering of the drugs in the IV. When Fremont finally responded, he *did* sound like an announcer, coming from a speaker way across the room. I was fading out.

"I sort of thought so. I've got great gaydar. Noel does too, and he just looked at photos of you. He said you're as gay as a box full of Speedos."

Fremont's breezy attitude sucked up all my paranoia. I laughed so hard my ribs hurt. I wound up coughing, bringing the gay nurse in to remind me to stay calm. Fremont promised he wouldn't make me laugh anymore. But the thing about the Speedos had lifted my mood vastly.

"Oh, God," I laughed. "I forgot how on point you are. Shit."

"What set you over the edge? You're not in the hotel because of work, are you?"

"No," I admitted, now quiet as a moonbeam. I looked around, to make sure no one was eavesdropping. "It's because I finally told Lauren I prefer men. She actually asked me first. Who knows how long it would've taken if she hadn't. I don't know, Fremont. I suddenly couldn't bear it anymore. I need to bust out of my shell. I need to at least *see* if it's the lifestyle for me."

"And looking for an online hookup gave you a heart attack?

"Yes."

In one motion, Fremont leaped from the chair to my bed, deftly avoiding the tubing and catheters, putting his arms around my neck. He nuzzled his face close to mine. Warm electricity flowed through my veins. Was this two men "hugging"? If so, I needed it. I needed it more than blood. With that one movement, Fremont erased the insult Dustin had done to me. I hugged him back with my one available arm. His hair was so silky against my palm.

He muttered, "Hunt. You did the right thing. You're not going to regret it. Come back with me to Havasu City. Come hang out at our clubhouse. There's a gay bar in town. You'll be with me and Noel and all our brothers." His words puffed warmly against my throat, making goosebumps rise on my bicep. "Look, we have a cook who'll give you all the right stuff to get your heart back in order. Brick cooks for lots of our guys who don't want clogged arteries." Fremont pulled back and looked me in the eyes. A hallowed haze seemed to fill the room just with his touch. "Believe it or not, lots of bikers pay attention to their health."

It seemed odd to feel myself smiling. "Brick? Didn't he get arrested for assaulting someone with a yogurt maker?"

Fremont smiled with fondness. "Yeah. That's my boy. Someone made some Native American cracks at him in a Bed Bath Beyond."

"But a guy was shot in the bedding section."

His smile did not fade. "Yeah. Good ol' Rover. Hey, we can take you to Sailor Jack's jackoff club."

Now my smile vanished. "What? That's a thing?"

"Yeah. Let's just say it's a private club where men can explore their desire for dick play."

A desire for dick play. That about describes me. "Wow. I don't know if I'm ready for that yet. Look what happened when I just DMd a guy."

Fremont sat up straight, but held my hand in his. "Oh, you were interested enough in a guy to actually DM? Send dick pics? I certainly don't want to stress you out. All in good time."

I looked across the room at a painting of a lighthouse. "Yeah. I was interested enough to ask him to meet." I chuckled just to lighten the mood. "IRL. NA."

Fremont frowned. "What does that mean? Well, don't look at that app until you're out of the hospital. Until then, I'll wait for you to be released. I'll bail you out of that Comfort Inn. You can follow me to Lake Havasu in your cage or whatever you drive."

"Cage?"

"Outsider's vehicle, a car."

"Oh. Yeah, I drive an electric Jaguar. Definitely a cage."

He squeezed my arm. "We'll have you fixed up in no time. I can see you in the saddle of a Dyna Wide Glide chopper with ape hangers."

"A *what?*"

"You'll look fantastic with that rock star hair flowing, those long legs, your boots on the foot pegs—"

"Boots?" I scoffed. "I wear high top tennis shoes."

Fremont patted my hand. "Just whatever you were doing when you got the heart attack, stop doing that."

"Reaching out to another man. Is this God telling me to stop that?"

Fremont made his mouth a thin line. "I tell you. Living with Father Noel hasn't made me any more cognizant about God's will. And I'm a Jew. My grandparents were incinerated in Poland in the holocaust. So no, I don't accept divine retribution."

"Jesus."

"But I can say this. You were scared. It scared you to reach out to that guy. *That* gave you the heart attack, not God. That and a bunch of lousy airfield food."

Many a time Fremont and I had walked to a roach coach and enjoyed greasy spoon items. So he knew. We didn't exactly order the salad, if indeed there were any at the barf buggies on our job sites. "Definitely scared. I asked if he wanted to meet in real life and he didn't answer right away, so I panicked."

"What was it that attracted you to that guy?"

"He was also from North Carolina."

Fremont flung up his hands. "Oh, mercy me, y'all! You reckon? Well, there you have it."

"That, and we had many similarities. He had a rough childhood. He got himself out of the hills, just like I did. Oh, and he's fucking hot as hell. He had a shirtless picture where he was fishing."

Fremont nodded with understanding. He and I had gone fishing several times too. "Okay. But I'm not bringing you a laptop until you're discharged into my care."

"Thanks, Fremont. Who knows? SoulWrestler is probably a massive ghettobilly. Probably just a scumbag player."

I had to hope that. The more I talked SoulWrestler down in my head, the less likely I'd be to feel I was missing out on something. He was a high school dropout, for one. Besides, if I got the balls to go to this jackoff club, I'd be a meat-eating meatpacker for the first time in seventeen years.

"SoulWrestler? Hm. Sounds like you have more in common than you realize."

Fuck Fremont.

CHAPTER FIVE

I was welding a set of FuBar tailpipes onto Jackie's Shovelhead.

Wearing a face shield that made me look like a space cadet, I saw movement from the corner of my viewing screen. I finished the seam and sat up straight. Jackie might be talking to me, and I needed to be responsive to his needs.

But his only need was to torment me.

"How's it going with the fag?"

I took off my shield and gave Jackie a blank face, hoping beyond hope he would just go away.

He didn't. "You know, the scientific fag. My back is so bad I've resorted to black market Oxycontin. Yeah, you heard right. *Oxy*," he spat. "It's making me loopy. I'm wide awake loopy."

I sat up straight. "Look, Jackie, I keep telling you you need to get some imaging done! Just think. You won't be able to fight in bars anymore if you keep this up. You'll need a back brace."

Jackie took two or three angry steps toward me, there in his condo carport. He must've thought better of kicking the ass of his mechanic, for he snorted and said, "No fucking hospitals! I just need some better meds, some Dilaudid or Percocet, whatever. Your boyfriend can hook us up with suppliers of the raw ingredients. We can put some trailer out there on my dad's land—"

"Yes!" I cried, practically getting up to my knees. "I keep telling you that! I can figure out how to make it, just give me the raw ingredients and a fucking trailer."

"All right, then! So how close you coming to reeling in that limp-wristed flamer?"

Shit. I had stepped right in it by offering to cook for him. My mouth was open in an *O*, but no sound came out. It had been fifteen days since StarGazer had ghosted me. Well, I hadn't even tried to look for the past six, that's how depressed it made me. I had made a purchase of Ruger 9mms and AK47 assault rifles with several thousand rounds of ammo that was way more power than we'd ever need. I just did it to bolster my mood. Now we didn't have any money for Jackie's imaging, as I had earlier bragged. But we sure had a shitload of iron that I now needed to protect from rivals and outsiders.

"Jackie, sir, I got your smokes."

The bartender Pinky saved me. She wore the same suspenders and vinyl-rimmed cap that she always wore in the bar, except now she smartened it up with a short corduroy jacket.

Jackie Daytona nearly tore the carton of smokes from her hand. "Ah, Pinky, I could kiss you." He fumbled getting a pack out, stripping the cellophane from it.

Pinky frowned. "Just your undying devotion is good enough for me." She squatted near me, fingers threaded between her knees. "A Fubar Alphabet 2-1, eh?"

I was surprised she knew the part. "Exactly. You know your bike stuff."

She shrugged. "I belong to a lesbian biker club. *Not nearly as badass as Society's Bag*," she yelled a bit louder for Jackie's benefit, "but these guys let us stay in town because, well, we're women. We're no one. We're no competition for them."

I glanced at Jackie to see if he was listening. Cigarette in mouth, he fumbled with a lighter. His hands shook like a rake with no leaves. "But you don't wear a cut, no colors."

"Jackie and Tyrone won't let me when I'm working. Come to our clubhouse if you get a free second. The Grease Pit over by Motel 66."

I was suspicious. Why did Pinky think I should come by her clubhouse? What did a bunch of lesbians have to offer me? But she seemed to be making the proposal with good grace, so I said, "Sure. Sounds good. I think I've seen it. Some naked legs . . . ?" I didn't want to discuss naked legs with a lesbian, and was glad when she filled in for me.

"Right, right, the stockinged neon legs, that's the place." Her eyes crinkled with kindness.

A '10 Road King pulled up in the driveway. I'd know those rumbling pipes anywhere because I had removed the baffles to make them louder. Good ol' Crosley Shelvador, erstwhile roommate of mine, flung his long leg over the saddle and sauntered forth with a paper bag in his grip. He took such long, happy strides I expected him to do a Dick Van Dyke over an ottoman. But he made it to Jackie's side safely.

"It's all here!" he reported. "Certified Angus chuck patty topped with aged white cheddar, balsamic glazed onions, and their secret sauce!" I wondered why, with a repertoire like that, Crosley couldn't assist me more in the kitchen.

Lit smoke jammed in his mouth, Jackie whipped the bag from Crosley's paw. The second he tore into it, he was ready with a put-down. "What the fuck, Shelvador? I asked for sweet potato fries, not these regular pieces of shit!"

I was actually surprised when Jackie shifted the bag into his left hand and gave Crosley an uppercut to the jaw. I'd seen much more powerful socks, to be sure, but Jackie also didn't have to do it at all. Is this what it was coming down to? Physical punishment for such small errors?

Pinky hissed in astonished air and half-rose to her feet. Crosley staggered back, arms flailing, stopped from falling on his ass only by an upright post. He jiggled his jaw with his palm, saying with shock, "But . . . it has arugula on it . . . "

Inhaling deeply of his nicotine, Jackie roared, "I've had it with all three of you losers! You fucking skidmarks are nothing but a pack of worthless toolbags!" Shoving the cig back halfway into his mouth, he swiped the dripping burger from the bag and tossed the unwanted fries at Crosley's face. It's safe to say we were all three hugely relieved when he turned on a dime and took the stairs to his condo two at a time.

"Whoa," said Pinky. "I've never seen him *that* wound up. That Oxy isn't doing him any favors."

"It's probably cut with a thousand fillers that don't help, either," I said, going over to Crosley to give a hand.

I could tell Crosley was different now, in some way. Jackie's outburst had already changed something in his brain chemistry. That, or he'd been prepared for this for awhile. A reptilian murkiness shaded his eyes, his nostrils flared, and for the first time I knew that Crosley Shelvador could be a very nasty customer.

He didn't bother knocking the fry off his shoulder. He addressed Pinky and me with a confidential yet unwavering tone. "I stabbed my girlfriend's mother in the chest twenty-eight times." His eyes flickered, and he glanced my direction. "She tried to give me a blowjob."

Pinky and I looked beseechingly at each other. *What in the name of fuck?* our eyes said. *What are we supposed to do with this information?*

It was a race to the finish between the friendly lesbian and me to see who would address Crosley first. Pinky beat me to it. "Wow, Crosley, that's pretty rough. This is like, uh, in your hometown?" She looked urgently back to me, panic in her eyes. We were both thinking *Where the fuck* is *his hometown, anyway?* I had not thought to pack my .45 while welding a tailpipe at the Sergeant-at-Arms' house. Crosley, however, had his piece stuck into the waistband of his jeans.

"Yeah, my hometown."

I said, "Which is . . . ?"

"Provo, Utah. I'm a Mormon. I'm a virgin, too."

"Oh, wow," Pinky and I said in tandem, genuinely sorry for the guy.

Crosley's face suddenly crumbled. "Fucking bitch! Why'd she have to do that? Who gives their son-in-law a blowjob, anyway?"

Pinky and I both thought *Mormons?*

Now he kicked some fries with his steel-toed boots. "Why, Crosley, why? The blood splashed from the cuts I made! She just burped and farted until she finally bought the farm." He closed his eyes as though recalling breathing lessons. *Breathe, breathe . . .* "When I get out of here, I'm going to be a serial killer."

Now Pinky clutched my arm, since Crosley wasn't looking at us. With our expressions and mouth positions, we figured out the best path to tread. This simple, unlikely fellow had morphed into a seriously damaged and quite possibly dangerous time bomb.

I tried to sound casual. "Wow, Crosley, what a story. What do you mean, 'when you get out of here'?

Turning to us, Crosley's jaw was set so firmly he seemed to snort boiling air. "You guys tell anyone any of this and you'll suffer the same fate as Flora."

"We understand," said Pinky. She elbowed me

I said, "I understand."

Crosley said, "I'm a tipster. You know? A stool pigeon."

Pinky and I were confused. She said, "An informant?"

"Right. That was part of my plea deal. They've been trying to infiltrate these fucking Society's Baggers for awhile now. They are seriously interested in Tyrone Shoelaces, but Jackie Daytona and Gangbang Greg are in their crosshairs, too."

Pinky exhaled. "Wow. Just wow. So they're gonna let you off scot-free if you give them the intel they want?"

Crosley exhaled too. The curtains on his eyes were raised, and in a flash he was almost back to his normal, dickwad self. He even tried to backhand my chest in a chummy way. "Yeah. Don't worry, Van the Man. We're not after you. We know you're only faking it."

Murderation! What had given me away? How much did Crosley know, or was pretending to know? Pinky and I exchanged frightened glances once more. I ventured, "Uh, what exactly do you mean? I seriously *want* to join this club."

Pinky backhanded me. "Aw, give it a rest, Van. I can tell you've got some secret agenda. I don't think you're in cahoots with the pigs like this yahoo here, but I don't think you just came from the backwoods hollers to ruin your life all over again with a one percent club like these condom breaths."

I narrowed my eyes at Pinky. As much as I yearned to confide, to lighten the load on my soul, I was also accustomed to secrecy. I admitted thinly, "You could say I'm not really a big fan, a big admirer of Tyrone and Jackie." I looked around the carport to make sure no one was lurking, eavesdropping. This paranoia made me ask Crosley, "Are you wearing a wire?" I'd never seen anything like that around Jefferson's clubhouse, especially not when Crosley busted shirtless into my room to ask me 'sup.

"Me? Not at the moment, though I've been known to. Look, you guys. I'm telling you, independent thinking like you-all do? There's no place for that in this club. These fuckers are running a terror campaign."

"Oh, don't I know it!" agreed Pinky. "Their brutality knows no limits. You should've been here when PJ and Squee played football with a stray cat in the back alley."

"Oh *God*, please!" I held up my hand to Pinky. "Brutality *does* have limits, and you just crossed it." I thought of the Persian cat who considered himself the owner of Claude and me. One day we were told he was on the side of the road, stiff as a furry statue. We didn't want anyone to see us holding a funeral for him. We'd be laughed out of town. We sobbed and clutched each other like the parents of a human baby.

Pinky defended herself. "I wasn't saying I *agreed* with it, Van."

"Then why do *you* stay here?" I asked her.

She shrugged. "They let us stay here. They protect us, in a way. I do it for my fellow sisters at the Grease Pit."

Crosley chortled. "Sexy lesbians. Girl-on-girl action." He was *definitely* back to his regular self.

"Look," said Pinky. "I just got my realtor's license before I was forced into tending bar for these jagovs. You think I want to stay in Needles? Now Lake Havasu, the Bent Zealots, there's a club for you, Van. You'd be right at home. You wouldn't be as conflicted and messed up as you are here."

Now *I* wanted to punch Pinky. *What makes her say I'd be at home in a gay biker club?* But Pinky continued.

"I'm butt buddies with Twinkletoes, a member in good standing of the BZ. I don't think they'd appreciate a narc like you, Crosley, but if Van here is in earnest about the biker life, I think they'd welcome you." She added with peculiar emphasis, "They're not *all* queer. Twinkletoes isn't. Brick isn't. Merwin Bigwater isn't. Lily Silverberry is. Or is she?" Pinky pondered, fingers on chin.

"*She*?" goofed Crosley. "There are *women* in this club?"

"Well, yes and no. Lily used to be known as Fred, or Fredericka. They're actually hang-arounds who run the club's pot store."

Crosley slapped himself in the forehead. "Oh my saints!" he said, echoing me. "What's the world coming to? Well, I have to finish my project here. Thanks for the offer though."

Pinky clipped, "No one's inviting you, Shelvador. I was talking to Van here. Get you out of the ATF's crosshairs. You're the one purchasing and hoarding all that iron. They'll be after you next. Society's Bags are criminals always. They don't rest or have a conscience or any shade of normal. Look what they're doing to you, Van. Making you catfish that poor scientist who just wants to find love."

I had to think. It *did* appear that StarGazer was merely trying to find some kind of solace with another man. As was I. I found myself blurting, "I'll tell you guys something. I'm not going to catfish that guy. I mean, I'll keep talking to him. But I'm not doing it for this fucked-up club." I neglected to say *why*, then, I was doing it. "These Baggers are animals, teaching you to never show fear. Any second they sense a shred of terror, a vibration of a tremor in us, and they'll pounce. I'll tell you,

Pinky. I didn't come to this club just to become a badass biker, although that part has kind of sucked me in. I've gotten too close to the animals, you know? But I really think, Crosley, that you and I have somewhat of the same goal."

"And what's that?" Crosley asked.

"I can't divulge that," I said, feeling a sort of pride in my spydom, my deep cover. "Let's just say it's retaliation for a deep wrong done to me by Tyrone and Jackie. I've been watching and waiting to pounce. Let's just say when it's my turn you won't see me again. Not even you, Crosley. So once more. I'm not the enemy. Keep your fucking ATF crosshairs off me."

"Deal," said Crosley. He was holding his fist out for me to bump, so I did, cornily enough.

Pinky said, "No one needs to laugh like the deeply fucked, Van. Come with me to the BZ fish fry."

I stuck out my lower lip. "Maybe I'll just take you up on that."

"You can drive. I haven't gotten up at nine in the morning since the last time I stayed out all night till nine in the morning."

We were all in cahoots now, sort of a club unto ourselves. All three of us jumped when the front door above slammed. Jackie Daytona was powering his way back to us, slapping his stupid shit kicking boots against the stairs.

"Rossi!" he barked, pointing at me like the Ghost of Christmas Yet To Come. "You done with that fucking tailpipe or what?"

"Yeah, yeah," I said, tearing my face shield from my skull. "You're good to go."

"Good, good." Snakes of dyed blonde hair squiggled over his stupid forehead. I needed to fast forward my game plan. But not in front of my new comrades, Crosley and Pinky. "Your next task is to get back to that fag. I want him up here pronto to our clubhouse."

"Well." I demurred. "We don't even know what kind of scientist he is. He might be an environmental engineer, dredging ponds. He might not know anything about drugs."

I expected what came next. He took three more seething strides toward me, flames dancing in the whites of his eyes. "We don't care about that anymore. We're going to threaten to out him to his work colleagues unless he comes to Jefferson's to give us all blowjobs."

What? Had I heard correctly? This club was straight as a flush, yet they'd all been discussing getting sucked off by another man, like it was a bullet item on their agenda? I said, "I presume I'm not to *say* this outright to him."

"No, no, course not. But that's how he's going to avoid us outing him to his workmates. How's it coming? You met with him in person yet?"

"Not at all! In fact, he ghosted me."

Pinky made an "aww" sound.

Jackie guffawed. "*He* ghosted *you*? You got ghosted by a fag? *Jesus*, Rossi, step up your game!" He looked about to slap me, like he'd done to Crosley. "We don't want any damned Prospect who can't reel in a poof."

With that, he grabbed his bike by the handlebars, kicked up the stand, and mounted it. As he rolled down the driveway and his engine cranked to life, the three of us shared looks.

Only Pinky dared to speak. "We better find him some new drugs."

CHAPTER SIX

Huntington

"**I** heard you planked in the middle of the main street."

Twinkletoes was modest. "Surprise Street. This is our burg, and we heard through the grapevine these asswipes were heading through our turf on some dumb fucking alleged Toys for Tots run. Yeah, right. You should see the Prez's house. Headless dolls, dogs chewing on toys, I mean, this is the shit they pretend to give kids? They keep all the money."

I was really warming to Twinkletoes. His bare arms were as thin as sugar cane, much like myself when young. Only Twinkletoes was probably thirty plus. I reasoned he couldn't have muscular dystrophy. Boys died at the age of twenty from that. Maybe ALS or myasthenia gravis. He sure seemed to get around, though.

"I heard they just rolled their rides right over your stomach." I knew enough to call bikes "rides." I was being steeped in biker lingo by Fremont and his lover, Noel. I had ridden "two up" down here from Tonopah, my thighs clamped around Fremont's muscular ones, thrust into a new world. A gay world of imagination, creativity, and intelligence. It was far, far wider and vaster than I'd expected.

And Twinkletoes wasn't even gay. How did he resist being surrounded by these buff, macho men? I had to guess he was just born that way. Poor downtrodden cisgender.

"Sure they did," Twinkletoes admitted, wiping his runny nose with the hand holding a beer cup. "If you distribute your weight correctly, you can avoid broken ribs and pelvis. I knew what I was doing. They fucking threw a crocodile right through the coffee drive-through window downtown!"

"Is that who Brick Mantooth was braining with a yogurt maker?" I asked.

Fremont explained to Twinkletoes. "Hunt here is a baby gay." It still sounded whacked to hear myself referred to as gay. I hadn't done the slightest gay thing so far, unless you counted that I currently wore a pair of striped velvet pants. It was just a holdover from my college rock star days. Women loved the way I dressed. "He's fascinated by the stories I've told him about you guys."

I sipped my beer while Twinkletoes hollered for Brick. Why was I surprised Brick was a Native American, a Navajo? There were several of them at the fish fry.

Twinkletoes said to Brick, "Hunt here wants to know why you brained that guy with the yogurt maker at Bed Bath Beyond."

"Oh." Brick puffed with pride. Though the incident had resulted in his arrest, it didn't seem to bother him. "Well, first, he played 'Highway to Hell' too loud on his device while browsing in the sheet department."

I asked, "Are you the one who shot him?"

"Oh, *no*," declared Brick. "That was a friend of his who got shot. He farted right there by some bedspreads and Rover just couldn't take it anymore. *Right, Rover*?" he bellowed through a cupped hand.

Rover was the most ploughed individual at the fish fry. He ambled over pigeon-toed, black hair tousled at the crown, ending in a buzzed fade. His eyes were so watery a teardrop ran down his face. Yet he wore the honorable colors of the Bent Zealots MC. "Oh, the farting guy? Yeah, I shot him in the ass. They were out of control and we were trying to buy — what was it again, Brick?"

"A yogurt maker."

"Right. A yogurt maker. We had a sudden yen to make yogurt. So I shot him in the butt."

Fremont reminded them, "Then the guy tried to hand the cop a taco as his ID."

Noel asked, "Was he from Florida?"

Everyone laughed full-throatedly at this, giving me pause for thought. Did I really want to get involved with characters like this?

Rover slurred, "So, doctor, I heard you're a doctor."

I stayed cautious. "Yes. A doctor of astrophysics." I always had to make sure people knew I wasn't a medical doctor, so they didn't start asking me about their irritable bowel.

Everyone made the appropriate round mouths. Rover poked his beer cup at me. "And you're an out and proud doctor of astrophysics?"

It was my turn to make my mouth an *O*. I had never confessed to anyone other than Dustin and my immediate family, of which Fremont was a part. But I had to start sometime, and the group surrounding me seemed perfectly amenable.

I said, "Yes, I believe so, though I'm just learning."

A guy named Dipstick toasted me with his cup. "You're a regular muscle bunny."

Everyone huzzahed for me, but this unfortunately piqued Rover's interest. Coming forward, he almost plastered his chest to mine, giving me what he seemed to think was a saucy look. "Oh, *yeah*? Why don't you say I practice on your flesh flute? I'm a virtuoso at interludes and refrains."

My nostrils flared at this smelly guy in my personal space. But a short lesbian, of which there seemed to be a few, quite literally stepped between us. She bumped him with her stomach and jabbed his chest with the vinyl brim of her hat and barked, "Back off, buddy."

Rover seemed so surprised, he really did back off. He even put his hands up in surrender. "Hey, hey," he soothed. "Didn't realize he was claimed by a fag hag."

"Hey," she warned, in her warm New York accent. "Watch who you're calling a fag hag."

"Yes," said a very feminine woman. The party was populated with "sweetbutts," straight women who liked hanging around gay men. The few hetero guys like Twinkletoes and Brick really scored with these ladies. "We get laid more than you do, Rover."

Fremont put a hand on my shoulder and steered me toward some fish smoke. The house belonged to the club's Prez and Veep, Turk and Lock—Lock Singer being the guy who'd led cops on a wild goose chase ending at an organ pipe cactus. Wrapped around hilly Paleozoic formations of limestone and rusty sandstone, the backyard of the mid-century house was spacious enough for the party of maybe a hundred. Kids, adopted by the members, clambered over rocks that had been smoothed by eons of seas rising and falling. A Bernese Mountain Dog stood guard and barked at them, in between catching mouthfuls of fish thrown by Bent Zealots. A Pomsky apparently named Todd followed the Berner everywhere, a little puffy shadow.

On one side of the patio, men in leather cuts shot baskets, clapping hands and clomping boots. On the other side they threw axes at a board nailed to the fence. These didn't seem like hazardous activities to their neighbors, apparently.

Everything was strangely out of balance from the parties I was used to. Women only made up about ten percent of the group. Eerie, yet somehow scintillating. I knew many of the men were paired up or even legally married to other men. I tried to view them just as a bunch of workmates, yet the stimulation of being in such a manly crowd had me on edge, all senses piqued.

In particular, I noticed a man standing behind the helpful lesbian clutching his red cup with nervous energy. He was ravishing in his tight T-shirt, pecs and biceps bulging. I can only describe his eyes as starry, a strange thing for StarGazer to think. They were an oceanic, powder blue shade, and he too seemed in awe of everything around him. Yeah, I shot a few glances at his crotch, packed nicely. I had to look away, or I'd get hard too.

He was not wearing a cut.

Instead, I talked to the lesbian. "Thanks for helping me out there."

Her words came rapid-fire, as if she were a standup comedienne. "I've had run-ins with that guy Rover. He's a major smack addict, and I didn't want to scare away any newbies. He's so oily. Like if you got on top of him you'd slide right off. Not all Bent Zealots are majestic centerfold material."

"Well, you helped out. And I'm definitely a newbie."

My heart thudded when she glanced at the oceanic guy. "That seems to be going around. Van, meet incredibly hot baby gay."

Being too manly to shake hands, we nodded at each other. I acknowledged my name. "Hunt." It was almost as though he asked me wordless questions, and I couldn't understand what they were. I addressed the butch to avoid his probing eyes. "What brings you here on a summer's day?"

She seemed bitter. "I sweat, smell like a bum, and want to murder people." She cheered up. "I do that every summer until it gets cold. Then I take a trip to Canada."

Van said, "Pinky here is a realtor. She's thinking of buying one of these houses and moving here." His voice curled around his words, dressed in the oldest American dialect of the Appalachias. I loved the Scots-Irish brogue, and in Van I saw a brother, rather than another ghettobilly in a backwoods holler.

I had been considering renting a house there, oddly enough. There was another federal missile range due east. I'd taken a leave of absence from my job, citing the heart attack. There was no homosexual future for me in Tonopah. I'd finally gotten up the nerve to take a peek again at Plugr, and SoulWrestler had asked me for a shirtless pic. I had no words. I'd been imagining we'd connected on some level, and was even willing to meet him IRL. The shirtless pic thing had turned me off, and I'd never responded back, or even looked at Plugr again.

The bad vibes around that whole incident helped temper my enthusiasm now. I nodded at Pinky. "I don't blame you. I think the same. These old mid-century Eichlers are a gold mine. And set against these red bluffs, all this reflective glass is like being on another planet."

Pinky grinned. "An astrophysicist would have a field day. Use me as your realtor and I'll give you a break on the commission."

"You're on," I said, as we both reached for our business cards.

Van said, "I don't blame Pinky for trying to get away from Needles. Not the best environment for someone as creative as her." Again, he barely glanced at Pinky. He was a rough mountaineer. His excellent snowy teeth told he hadn't been down and out in Appalachia, but he was tough enough to take a man to the ground with his bare hands. He sparkled his eyes at me.

Fremont broke in then. "Yeah, Pinky has earned protection by a rival club of ours. There's something wrong with those fucking Society's Bag members. I mean, more wrong than your normal one percent club."

It took me a few seconds to realize that Fremont looked suspiciously at Van. It seemed to take Van a few moments, too, until Pinky elbowed him. She even had to respond for him.

"Van here's just a welder. A baby gay, like your men said. He comes and, ah, welds stuff for us at The Grease Pit, our boi hangout." She flipped my business card between her fingers. "You work at the Tonopah Test Range?"

Did my card say that? I had to think. No, it just named my company, a subcontractor to the government. But it did say Tonopah. "Yes," I admitted guardedly. It seemed many people in this backyard had a lot to hide. Maybe Fremont had told her. Though as a frequent test range employee himself, he knew not to advertise that. "I look through telescopes, guard the country from stray space junk."

"Unidentified aerial phenomenon. Or incoming missiles," Fremont filled in.

"That too," I admitted with a toss of the head.

Van butted in unexpectedly. "You gaze at stars," he said with wonderment.

"Sometimes," I said, and then remembered my StarGazer name. Could I have tussled with this welder on Plugr? The odds were seriously against it. Although I did use my real photo . . .

Pinky shook my hand with her rock-hard grip. "It's a deal, Dr. Mountjoy. I'll only charge you two percent, and we can become familiar with these beautiful homes together."

I liked Pinky Epstein, her suspenders, and her New York accent. "Deal," I agreed, and Pinky took me back into the house, to the low electric stovetop, the exposed wooden beams, the colorful pressboard kitchen cabinets.

Pinky bubbled. "Don't you just feel like you're Don Draper holding a glass of scotch listening to Miles Davis on your phonograph?"

I didn't feel quite that groovy. "More like Darrin Stevens listening to Peter, Paul and Mary." It was a giant move for me to make. I wasn't even certain my company would allow me to transfer to Aubrey Peak. I figured I'd play on their sympathy, make it out like after my heart attack I wanted something less challenging. But if it was true that the stress of coming out had given me the heart attack, I certainly wasn't helping things moving to Rough and Ready.

With a biker gang.

Sorry, biker club.

She said, "Now, let's see if they updated the air conditioning . . . none of these homes came with it . . . "

My phone buzzed a strange tone. I remembered I'd put some kind of alert on Plugr to let me know anything urgent. So far, it had only buzzed once, when I hadn't realized I'd stood up DapperDeveloper with a big white cock, who somehow thought we had an NSA assignation at Best Western in Bullhead City. Did the IT developer think we had another imaginary hookup?

Fucking murderation. It was SoulWrestler, and he frantically apologized for the shirtless request.

> CLAUDE: *I'm so sorry about the shirtless thing, Star. I just could not resist, my hunger for you is so strong. I'm not that kind of guy, really. Your soul has penetrated me far deeper than any of these other players. Please tell me you'd still like to meet IRL.*

I was speechless. If y'all want to know, I was sort of angry. That Tar Heel had the mind to urgently message me two weeks later? Then I recalled, it was *I* who hadn't responded, mostly due to the heart attack. I might've laughed off the shirtless thing, maybe even been a bit flattered by it. So now, just to prevent Pinky from asking questions, I quickly tapped back.

> HUNT: *I'm not in Tonopah anymore. I'm in Lake Havasu at a fish fry with a bunch of gay bikers.*

That was it. Confident I'd at least thrown Soul for a loop, I replaced my phone in the holster and followed Pinky to the garage to examine the water heater. I would let his apology — half-assed or not — sink in. There was no rush to hook up with Soul when there was a house full of juicy prospects already within reach.

It happened when I went back outside to take a look at the water meter. A flurry of activity in the red sand of the back forty, and the Bernese Mountain Dog was off like a shot chasing a cat.

"Korg! Korg, come!" shouted Turk and Lock, almost in tandem. "Korg, *no!*"

But Korg was having none of it. He'd backed the silky — now bristly — cat into a sandstone hollow, barking his giant head off. Bikers clambered up the rolling rock formations, bellowing pointlessly at the dog. Rover folded his arms and laughed. The most amazing thing? The swiftest of all was Van. He scrambled like a hunting spider up those gritty hillocks, reaching the cat in a flash. He even shoved aside a couple bikers in leather vests to be the first.

"Van, *no!*" yelled Pinky, as though he were another rowdy dog.

The second Van lunged for the cat as though he'd scoop it in his arms, I was off, too. It was one of those thoughtless actions, like seeing your child about to be smashed by a bus. You just do it.

A biker named Berkeley was shouting, "That's one of my mom's cats that escaped!" just as the scared feline yowled and raked claws down Van's muscular forearm before darting off.

Van and I were practically neck and neck chasing that damned cat. Lauren and I had a nice cat for about twelve years the kids named Leo. It was a good enough cat, and moved with us through many homes and towns. I was cat-friendly, I guess. At least, that was my motivation at first.

We easily hopped the short property fence and were in the wild. We zipped past groupings of spiky agave and ducked beneath rust red manzanita branches. The cat was still within range, so we pressed on.

I didn't think too hard about how to actually *catch* the cat. Logically, we'd just get scratched all to hell like Van had just done. Does anyone ever really *catch* a cat, without the help of a net? Fencing gloves might've helped us.

If catching the cat was our real plan.

I found out later it was an ocotillo that tripped us up. I don't know who went down first, Van or me. But we skidded on our chests across the prickly branches, digging trenches in the sand like downed rockets. We veered to a stop against a little wall of sand and thorns, one jammed half an inch into my throat, one in my palm.

And Van was on top of me, clenching my ass cheek between his thighs.

CHAPTER SEVEN

Van

Bless Stargazer's heart.

He really put himself out there, elbowing serious bikers out of his way to chase down this migrant Maine Coon cat with me. We'd fallen to the ground together in a tangle of buff limbs, our pectorals pumping, my swollen dick hard against his ass.

And he made no effort to get away.

We huffed and puffed, Stargazer's exquisite face turned away from me. He could not see the predatory expression on my face. I'd been focused on hunting down the escaped cat — he brought to mind the fluffy feline Claude and I had owned, found stiff on the road shoulder, and I was determined this one not suffer the same fate.

The stunning astrophysicist had kept up with me, long legs pumping, barely panting as we leaped to avoid cacti and bushes. It was as though we journeyed on this obstacle course, every damned ocotillo on the planet getting in our way, jabbing spines into our thighs. Just knowing I ran with my archangel by my side spurred me on. The cussed cat was on a rock one second, or waiting for us in some ground critter's hovel the next, but always one leap ahead of us. I didn't see StarGazer — Hunt — glance once at me, but I knew there was a reason for his crazy dash.

Did he recognize me as SoulWrestler? Of course not. I hadn't once used my real photo. I'd utilized the pictures of my lover Claude Berger — the one solitary reason I'd come to Needles in the first place. No, Hunt could never have imagined I was the guy behind the shirtless pic request, the fellow Appalachia ghettobilly of Hank's Hot Springs' hottest meth-making op. The raggedy mountaineer just lusting after his angelic muscle bunny self. Oh man, how I'd longed to rub my face against those squiggling, silken locks! To run my tongue past his turquoise necklace and take the nubbin of his nipple into my mouth. To slide my hands around the small of his back, pressing his crotch to my chest. I could rasp him to the brink of orgasm just with the power of my pectorals. The crown of his big cock bursting from his zipper would be enough for me to jizz inside my own jeans.

Now we somehow stumbled in our quest. Who tripped who I can't say. All of a sudden, we were falling headlong in a tumbleweed of limbs. I know I bruised at least one knee and a shin, maybe banging against one of Hunt's. When we slid to a stop, his shapely ass was pinioned between my thighs, and my dick plumped against him.

No one made a move to separate our bodies.

He must've felt my dick twitch. I barely noticed the cat sprinting off toward the suburban homes. Now the only reason we were mashed together against the khaki sand was to finally, at long last, melt together in the sexual union that was our fate.

I steadied my palms against the ridge of soil we'd raised up, and lifted my torso a few inches. This jammed my pelvis against his gluteus even more firmly. To strengthen my intent, I placed one palm against his other ass cheek and squeezed. Fucking heaven. Firm and muscular, as I'd suspected from the photos he'd posted. StarGazer next to a telescope, the flat plane of his lower back sloping into the shapely, juicy ass. His starry eyes sparkling, his bear claw necklace drawing my eyes to a tantalizing unbuttoned shirt that let me see nothing.

He squirmed over to face me, flinging one arm passively onto the sand above his head. Oh my saints, his bowed cupid lips, his exquisitely pointed nose and yes, those diamond eyes questioned me.

His words almost shocked me stone cold.

"Who are you?"

His syrupy, dripping holler accent sounded just like me.

I was too scared to reply. Had he somehow already figured out I was a shirtless Claude Berger fishing in the dazzling sun? Hunt kissed me first.

He flung his other arm around my neck, pulling me down to him. He plastered his hot mouth to mine, blatantly experimenting. Sucking and licking my lips, he seemed to sigh inwardly, as though this was what he'd been seeking. And why not? I was buff and desirable, so I got ahold of myself and kissed him back.

I slipped my tongue inside his mouth. We licked and sucked on each other, snorting scorching breaths against each other's faces. I groaned when I bit his bowed upper lip. It was a drug I'd been craving for so long, since the arduous task of weaning myself from the glories of meth. I wedged a thigh between his, and his long muscular legs separated willingly. His pulsing hard-on throbbed against my hip, and I found I was kissing him passionately, almost with love. He kissed me the same way.

Van Rossi couldn't be seen acting passionate anymore! Passion was for losers, guys who got their heart broken when someone died. No, I was Claude Berger, built fisherman who just drove a delivery truck to make straight bank to fund his lustful encounters, no strings attached. Claude was drug-free and masculine, and Claude would break that kiss immediately!

So I did. I raised my torso and looked down at him, his heavily lidded eyes almost crossing with a sensual craving. I admit I did spear my fingers through some of his silken locks. It was just too tempting. But I quickly turned this steamy action into a brutal one. I lifted his head as I lifted his torso, and I flipped him over.

I growled in his ear. "This is what guys like you are made for. This is what you've been fucking craving for so long."

We kneeled together in the sand as I dry humped him. I gripped his narrow hips and wedged my erection against his ass crack. Just the thrill of contact surged up my prick, and I reckon I spurted a couple drops inside my fucking pants.

"How did you know?" he said.

I cupped his Adam's apple in my palm and fingered his necklace chain. I couldn't resist taking a snarling bite from his neck. I smelled musk, sweat, and maybe coffee. "I know guys like you," was all I said, squeezing the turquoise pendant between my fingers.

My other hand explored the ridges of his abdomen. Yanking his shirt from his striped pants, I gasped with wonder at the contact. Skin on skin. I savored the moment, the seconds when I had the utmost control over Hunt, when I could do virtually anything I wanted. I nibbled on his earlobe, decorated, almost predictably, with a turquoise stud. I thumbed the sinewy abs, my other hand dropping to finger his nipple, hard and tight.

"Damnation," I growled in my thickest hill people voice. "You're set to be one of the sexiest men I've ever tangled with."

He blurted, "I can say the same about you."

With that, I could control myself no more. My hand slid beneath his belt buckle and gripped the hard trunk of his cock. My other hand undid the buckle and buttons swiftly, like a cartoon where the metal discs go flying. I squeezed the bulge of his cock from outside the fabric, just enjoying it for the moment before I let it spring free. Oh my saints he was hung, thick as well as long, meaty, and delicious.

I had to restrain myself. I couldn't pin him down and drill him up the ass. No. Not yet. If we were both going to live in Havasu, there'd be plenty of time. Time to build up the suspense, the eroticism, the pure hunger and delight in exploring each other. No. I had to have technique, control, discipline.

So I let his cock jump free. "Ah!" he cried when I gripped his burning meat in my palm. I began a dry, tactile pumping of that cock.

He, too, had spurted a few drops of jizz, and I palmed it around the tight mushroom head to grease up his tool. No one can possibly know the lust that surged up my dick as I dry humped this stud. I was really afraid I would come inside my pants. How fucking lame would that look? I had to restrain myself, a next to impossible task, and concentrate on the cock at hand.

"You're a fine, gorgeous muscle bunny," I snarled in between sucks to his earlobe and jugular. He arrowed his fingers through my short-cropped, curly hair, fingering the sweat popping from my skull. He squirmed, encouraging my hard-on in his asscrack. His throat resonated with satisfied murmurs, almost like he was singing a tune along to the rhythm of my hand pumps.

Cupping his balls, I massaged them almost brutally as I jacked him. "You're just a delicious stud. You a bottom? You're a nice, sexy bottom, just juicy, beautiful, like a stunning angel. Your dick is mouthwatering. I can't wait to get it in my mouth."

Hunt's mouth hung open in a concentrating *O*, gasping and gulping as he neared orgasm. He probably wasn't aware that his fingernails dug into the back of my neck. I didn't care if blood ran down my shoulders. I was gonna jack this angelic stud into the middle of next week, until he jizzed against that prickly pear cactus we'd nearly slid into.

I could make out some of his words. "Damnation . . . hunger for you . . . raggedy . . . oceanic . . . "

Did that mean he liked me, or didn't like me? I had to not give a fuck as I continued pumping him into oblivion. I moved my hand that stimulated his balls up the ridges of his abs and to his pec. He had a glossy smattering of hair decorating his admirable flesh, and when I pinched a nipple as I'd been longing to do, it set him right off.

He gasped and held his breath. My fingers felt the semen explode up the underside of his penis, ejaculating out the slit with shocking speed. Damnation, he really *did* nail that prickly cactus with his swift jet. His fingers dug deeper into my shoulders as he arched his back, his ecstatic jizz festooning the spiny fruit. And yeah, when he arched his back like the cat we'd been chasing *I* lost it, and resumed pumping into his shapely ass, grinding him into smithereens until yeah, okay, I admit it, I finally came a little in my pants.

Who could have helped it? This archangel was in my hands, willing, a submissive bottom. I could've nailed him to the sand right then and there, but I didn't. I just provided him with rapturous, man-on-man action — and if any of those fucking Bent Zealots were watching, more power to them. *I* was the one commanding the action. *I* had this sensuous stud literally in the palm of my hands.

No one needed to know I was creaming in my pants, I was so hot for Dr. Mountjoy.

Hunt

Who *is this guy?*

What did he possess that allowed him to manhandle me so brutally in the middle of an empty desert? We were drenched in sand and sweat and this guy had the boldness to dry hump me so my erection made an impression in the fucking sand.

And I let him.

This fucking redneck jacked me off with lustful precision.

And I let him.

No, I more than fucking let him. I *encouraged* him by rolling my ass against his giant hard-on, arching my back, jutting my cock into his hand. We were so brazenly displayed there in the sand like a glorious statue, my penis naked to all eyes, if only the view of this curious whitetail deer.

I hadn't had this satisfaction of my skin hunger since college, and Van's talented fist frigged me into oblivion fast as a fisher can let out line.

It was fucking superb reveling in this guy's hard body, his pecs working against my shoulder blades, his swollen erection shoved into my ass crack. Because he sounded Appalachian like SoulWrestler. My fellow peckerwood who had dragged himself out of the holler, gotten clean, and turned to the admirable career of delivery driver. Lifted weights, from the looks of things.

And now stroked me to ecstasy.

I knew I uttered some fragments of words. There was something about the ocean in his eyes, and my eternal skin hunger, my longing to be touched. When he slid a hand from my balls to my nipple, I came like an exploding firecracker. I shot maybe six feet, until a cactus dripped with my seed.

And I didn't care.

Fact, I loved it.

This white trash rube was seducing *me*, an educated scientist. And I admired the lewd pattern of my dripping come on the spines of the succulent.

I shuddered massively, gasping like a sobbing child. I think my lower lip even trembled. The release was monumental, a seismic shift in my entire psyche. I was in the hands of a hillbilly stranger, his every stroke causing my knees to weaken with gratitude. But who was really in control? Van was the one who wanted *my* cock. He purported to be the aggressor, but didn't *my* reaction control *him*? Was he the alpha, and I the beta? Perhaps I was a gamma, an unusual hybrid of the two, topping from the bottom, as they say. Gamma rays were the most harmful rays of all. They can pass through a man, ruining cells as they go.

Perhaps Van wasn't the hazard to me. I was the hazard to him.

Eventually, I stopped coming. Though I was still putty in his hands, he pulled away abruptly as though searching for a place to wash up. Without his buff torso cradling me, I collapsed into a praying position, panting. I felt so completely drained of thoughts. I really had no next step in mind. Nothing like this had ever happened to me before. I was only cognizant enough to stuff my throbbing cock back into my striped velvet pants that now seemed like such an arrogant affectation.

Oh. That was a thought. I was an arrogant asshole.

"Hey," said Van in a kind tone. I looked up to see the towering monolith that was his silhouette blocking the sun. He reached a hand down to me! "That was, ah, excellent. You're even hotter than I hoped. Cumon. Get up."

When we were at eye level—amazing, he was exactly the same height as me, six two—I could barely tolerate facing him. When had I become so shy, so stuttering? Maybe when my mother would call me a fag because I was tall, lanky, and awkward. Now I was tall, muscular, and awkward. My mother's voice still echoed in my head.

Being more experienced than I, Van spoke first. His eyes didn't waver from my face. He was bold—one might even say cocky. "That was great. I'd like to see you again. But you live way . . . ah, up north in Nevada somewhere?"

"Tonopah," I admitted. "I'm considering moving here."

Man, his smile was dazzling. How were his teeth so white, especially crawling out of the holler? "Me too! I really hate Needles. I want to make a clean break with some people."

Why did I feel so crushed that he was involved with "some people"? All I could say was, "Yeah. Me too. Hey, let's find that fucking cat. Who was that guy shouting that it was his mother's?"

When he grinned, dimples appeared. "Berkeley. His mother had a house down the street, completely hoarded up. Shopping channel and junk. Pinky told me. He's a new club member."

I shrugged. "Maybe we can find his cat for him."

Van shrugged too. "Maybe we can."

And we turned back toward the Prez and Veep's house, I realized Van still held my hand. I casually let mine drop. "We can lure it with food. Chasing it would never work."

"Yes," said Van. "Luring is way better than chasing."

CHAPTER EIGHT

Van

"Tyrone knocked a hole in his bathroom wall so he can watch the street while he showers."

Pinky took this news from Crosley with a matter-of-fact nod. "Yeah. They have a new saying. 'Viva Society's Bag, and cornhole the rest.'"

I banged my beer mug on the cocktail table. The three of us had met at The Grease Pit, Pinky's clubhouse, for a confab on recent events. There was increased blathering about the Society somehow "getting" the Bent Zealots. I didn't think anyone knew Pinky and I had been to their fish fry, although I was panic-stricken they'd find out. Tyrone and Jackie singled the Zealots out for their particular brand of abuse. They loathed those homos, yet they wanted me to catfish StarGazer into coming to Jefferson's and blowing all of them?

I had to step up my game. Finally achieve what I'd come here to do.

I had to cap those dudes.

I said, "Their philosophy is better to be feared than admired. Nine-tenths of them are Filthy Few members." The Filthy Few was an extra patch any one percenter was allowed to add to his cut once he'd murdered someone in cold blood. *Hey. I guess I'll get to wear one soon.*

"Yeah," said Crosley. He hadn't stopped eyeballing the lesbians since we'd arrived there. He kept wiggling his eyebrows at them, as though they were about to sit on his lap. Fact, quite a few of them frowned at him with disgust.

Most of them were of the suspendered variety, like Pinky, manly to the point of having a few facial hair growths. Many wore lumberjack shirts buttoned to the chin, some adorned with ties. A couple of wives appeared cisgender at first, their slim bods tucked into pleated dresses. But upon closer inspection, one of these women had hairy legs and balls.

So no, Crosley was barking up the wrong tree, his radar off the track. "Yeah," he said, "the only one who hasn't killed anyone is George Zip."

Pinky shook her head with sorrow. "George Zip," she pronounced, as if his name was synonymous with "chump." "He was knocked unconscious in the Lion's Club men's' room with a silver buffet tray."

"Yeah," said Crosley, reminiscing fondly. "It was still full of cocktail sauce. Looked like a spree killing in there. Hey, what happened to your arms, Van the Man? Looks like you've got cat scratch fever."

He referred to the foot-long scratches that Maine Coon had given me at the fish fry when I tried to embrace it. I ignored him, putting the finger back on Society's Baggers. Their actions created an amazing body count. "Don't forget that couple they shot to death last week in the movie theater."

Pinky got heated. "Yeah, because they wouldn't stop texting. Tyrone and Jackie were trying to watch that Borat movie."

I said, "The part with Guiliani and his pants zipper. Tyrone said 'You fuck with one, you fuck with all of us.'" I mumbled, "People have been flipping me off on the road, jamming past me because of the colors I sport."

Pinky turned to Crosley. "Speaking of zippers, how's it coming on the, you know, the sting? I'm like an ant under a magnifying glass here, bartending for them. Fried to a crisp."

Crosley abruptly turned into the wannabe serial killer right before our very eyes. He crunched neatly on a potato fry—never a sweet potato fry after his run-in with Jackie Daytona—and clipped, "I'm-a tellin' you, we're gettin' them all on murder charges. Don't worry, Van—we're ignoring the gun running stuff because it's small change."

"Oh, good," I said. I'd been wondering about that. "I was even thinking of taking some of the iron with me to the Zealots, as sort of a peace offering."

Crosley shrugged. "Be my guest. You're in charge of all of it. But don't take it before tonight."

"Why?" I asked, feeling ominous.

Again, Crosley looked from side to side as we all leaned in. "There's an event tonight. Red wings."

"What's that?" spat Pinky.

"How come I wasn't told?" I whined. I'd been feeling left out of a few things lately, a few runs where they'd told me to stay put and clean the kitchen or whatever. Then I'd wondered why I felt left out of a club that needed to be wiped off the face of the earth.

"Here," said Crosley, lifting up a couple fingers to get someone's attention. "Let's just hear what Marcel has to say about red wings. Oh, Marcel!" he trilled.

She was a slender dyke wearing a dress coming forward with a curly smile. I could tell she wore a wig, as the shiny curls were too perfect to believed, and she slopped the makeup on with a trowel. She put a hand on Crosley's shoulder.

He said, "Tell my friends what red wings are."

Marcel recited, "Red wings is cunnilingus with menstruating women. It's done in some MCs as a rite of passage for Prospects to become fully patched."

Now that Crosley didn't need her, he waved her away. I saw by the softening of his features he was turning back into a doofus. He got in a slap on Marcel's butt as she tiptoed off in her heels. "So there you have it."

Pinky gazed at me with a horrified lifted lip. "Eating out women on the rag? I'm a *lesbian*. And even *I've* never done that."

I splayed my hand on my chest. "I've never heard of it." Something struck me. "Wait a minute, Crosley. *Prospects*? *Prospects* means me and you."

Crosley folded his hands together behind his neck as though waiting for the Niners to come onto the field. "It sure does, buddy. It sure does."

"Oh *ho!*" I shouted. "Wait just one fucking second! I ain't got no desire to stick my face between a woman's bloody thighs!"

Pinky mumbled, "Or *any* woman's thighs."

"Hey look!" Crosley protested. "I have to do it too. Tyrone said he'd do it just to show us how tough he is."

I yelled, "Why do I get the feeling you'd *enjoy* it? Hey, Marcel!" I half-stood, uncaring how many heads turned toward me. "Marcel! Who's the volunteer from the Grease Pit for this event?"

She fluttered her eyelashes at me. "Why, me."

"Wait a minute, wait a minute." I waved her back over, and she came with pigeon toes, clomping in her platform shoes. "Now tell me what's in this for you. Do you get some special patch from your club?"

Pinky sneered. "I'll bet we just *avoid* being run out of town on a rail. Is that it, Marcel?"

"That's basically it. I'm just doing the club a favor."

I was thoroughly disgusted. "All right, get out of here," I moaned, and sank back into my chair. "*Red wings.* This is the fucking limit."

Pinky backhanded me. "You've got to be more aggressive, Van. I know you can do it. If this is your limit, then *show* them. I know you've got something up your sleeve. Please don't tell me, because I don't want my realtor's integrity compromised. But I've got a feeling you should do it now."

I held my forehead in my fingertips. "I know, I know," I moaned. I'd been fixing to send those two greaseballs six feet under but the fact of the matter was, I'd been chickening out. Yes, *chickening out.* I'd gotten too close to the animals—I'd become one of them.

Crosley egged me on. "I know you're here for a reason, Van. You came out of nowhere, from those hill people in South Carolina."

"North," I corrected him.

"North," he agreed. "You came from the Blue Ridge Mountains and just popped up at our door, saying you knew a lot about bikes and could weld stuff."

"I *can* weld," I said between gritted teeth.

Oblivious, Crosley continued. "But what do we know about your past? You should've made a fancy backstory like I did just to make it look good."

Pinky crinkled her face. "*What* backstory? We just found out you're a Mormon."

Crosley protested. "I've got a *huge* backstory. I'm a thug from Alberta, Canada—that way they wouldn't know I'd made up the club."

"Oh yeah?" asked Pinky. "What's that, the Mons Venus Riders?"

"No," said Crosley, clearly not aware what Pinky meant. He sat up straight. "The Cruising Chubbies."

Pinky guffawed. "You wanted to draw attention to the fact that you were all fat?"

"Well," harrumphed Crosley, "no one was really *fat*, since the club was made up."

Pinky slapped the table with her palm, making one of those soundless laughs, but I really couldn't join in. I was too busy having flashing bright crimson nightmares about sticking my face between a woman's legs. Any legs. Even legs that weren't red or winged.

Fact was, my showdown with Tyrone and Jackie was way overdue. It was now or never.

I started to shove off from the cocktail table when Crosley blarted, "Pinky, you're friends with the Bent Zealots. I just heard talk Tyrone plans to jump them during that Kingman run next month. Pull their patches."

Pinky froze. "Take their colors?"

I'd heard of that. It was a way of putting another club to shame. Yet the Zealots' range was enormous, spanning from

Laughlin to Havasu, down to and including Quartzsite and the Colorado River rezzes. Yes, biker turf could absorb the native lands, if they had agreements with them. I'd seen more than a few Navajo at the fish fry. Pinky told me they'd done a lot of good for the natives, run druggies off their lands, erected monuments, saved dogs — saved some of the kids now in the club.

Crosley said, "Yeah. They want to make a statement and steal their bikes on a crowded street, so everyone sees what they did." He switched gears as he crunched popcorn in one cheek, squirrel-like. "I probably shouldn't have told you that. But we're out to get Baggers for murders. If we can stop some future ones, all the better."

"I hear ya," said Pinky.

I didn't hear him. I *wanted* to commit future murders. I stood all at once like a spring unfurling and said, clear as I could muster, "I'm going back to the clubhouse to make pizzas."

Pinky called after me, "Make sure not to put too much *tomato sauce* on the *dough*."

I caught her meaning, but wasn't about to stray from my goal. Running into StarGazer — Dr. Mountjoy — at the fish fry had done me in. He was moving to Rough and Ready, so *I* was moving to Rough and Ready. There were no two ways about it.

There weren't really any pizzas to make — Tyrone had told me to order a variety to be delivered to their mysterious event at PJ and Squee's house that night. Instead, I went to the storage unit where we kept the most iron. I admired the brand new AK-47 assault rifles, running my fingertips down their sleek wooden stocks. I had a stash of Ruger 9mms. Then there were the Sig Sauers, the .40 cal pistols. The slow-moving, knockdown .45 ACPs.

I selected one of those, shoving it down my waistband and covering it with my cut. I was the one taking inventory, and the sole spreadsheet was on my phone. Once I buried

Tyrone and Jackie there would be no time to race back to the storage unit and carry off iron, so I had to make my move now. I still had the Econoline van I'd driven cross country in, stashing about half the entire storage unit in the back. Not the best position to be in should I be pulled over by pigs—or shot at by a raving Society's Bagger—or, I should say, a random enemy of the Bag. It was my only choice if I wanted to make it intact to Rough and Ready . . . and the desire of my heart.

Dr. Mountjoy was looking to find The One. That scared me, but in a way kept me going back for more. Before we had returned to the fish fry and the farce we were just barely strangers, I'd pulled him into Turk and Lock's little fence and laid a giant, open-mouthed kiss on him. Damnation, that fiery scientist gave as good as he got. He'd jizzed all over a cactus in a gravity-defying stunt, but his luscious, big prick was stiff again as he grabbed a handful of my ass and ground into me.

That time we were wild and sloppy. We snorted hot puffs against each other's faces while lapping at fat tongues. It was a way of tasting StarGazer—*my StarGazer, how did I get him in my arms?*—and leaving his primal imprint on my cells.

Sure, a few bikers probably saw us. Big deal. What were they going to say? They probably wished they were us.

When we broke it off, we staggered back from each other a few steps. Dazed and confused, our eyeballs swimming in our heads. The sheer force of our lust had taken us by surprise. Hunt started to stutter something, but I saved him from it.

"Let's talk to Berkeley about his mom's cat."

"Shu—shu—" Hunt sputtered. "Sure," I think he meant to say.

So we got back into party mode, and stole fleeting glances at each other like some sappy peckerwoods. It was all right. Kind of exciting in a way. A tremulous energy flooded me, like the first days of Claude. Sure, we made meth in Hank's Hot Springs in a trailer behind a fancy house, a couple of Barcaloungers on the lawn, not bathing every day. But we helped dig neighbors out of the snow, we never chained up dogs, and we adopted a cat named Mighty. And our hot and bothered lovemaking was secreted away in chambers of the big empty house. We'd stumble out wild-eyed to sell product to guys who had missed a few dental appointments. I had a parallel life.

"What's the cat's name?" I asked Berkeley.

Berkeley didn't seem to know much about his mother. She had gone into hospice by the time he'd arrived back here from art school. And with her herd of a hundred cats, he had to admit he didn't know the Maine Coon's name.

"Mighty," I suggested.

"Mighty," laughed Hunt. "I like that."

I parked the gun van in an industrial area of town and took a Lyft back to Jefferson's, where my ride was already in the alley. My laptop was a perfect fit in my saddlebag, along with my earthly possessions—a couple pairs of jeans, some photos of Claude, and that corny book, *Zen and the Art of Motorcycle Maintenance.* I don't know why I'd been carrying it around for years. Claude had given it to me. At first we thought it was really about motorcycle maintenance. But now I liked the Zen parts.

I took the Queen poster. I'd really grown to think of Dr. Mountjoy as a secret Brian May in an alternate life. Fremont had told me that the good doctor had been a guitarist in a band in college—Princeton, no less. *I jacked off a brainy hunk from Princeton.* I was actually starting to get a sense of self for the first time since Claude died. *I must really be someone.*

Taking a look around the stale cigarette atmosphere of Jefferson's bar, I thought of the time Tyrone Shoelaces had snarled at me, "If I find out there's a narc in this clubhouse, he's buried." He dry fired his pistol at the wall to make his point.

Another time, a manic Jackie Daytona growled in the general direction of myself, Crosley, Pinky, and a few other lackies. "People I don't personally know are going to be roadkill." My nights at the club all blurred together in images of beer mugs, fists, and spit. Only the presence of Pinky and Crosley lately had kept me from truly losing it.

I was about to truly lose it now.

Claude Berger . . . Claude Berger . . . I do this for you.

I didn't want to get pulled over—or otherwise spat upon—so I rode sedately to PJ and Squee's 1950s tract house. I don't know how the working class neighborhood tolerated the blaring, tinny music, the constant roar of tailpipes coming and going, and the general shouting of the usual crowd. Not to mention the stink.

The burned fuel emanating from my tailpipes didn't even overwhelm the reek of dogshit as I parked my ride one house down, for a quick getaway. I even pointed it in the direction of the Colorado River, which I planned to follow on my journey to Rough and Ready. Once again, I'd be a nomad, but this time, I had a path.

I fluttered my tight T-shirt over the piece stuck into the back of my jeans, and headed to the door. *What a clusterfuck.* I had to dodge the snarling pit bulls chained near the door and clamber over a shitfaced PJ. Master of his own domain, he greeted people at the door by hazily lifting one hand, but otherwise acting as a doormat. *Nice way of getting out of redwings.*

I lifted my chin in greeting to Tyrone Shoelaces wearing a metal stormtrooper helmet, holding court in the kitchen and lecturing some hang-arounds. I couldn't reckon the manner in which he returned the nod. Was he all-knowing, all-seeing? Had Crosley tipped him off to my alleged plan? Tyrone had always given me the jitters, the way he fought without offense or reason. I swore he gave me an evil side-eye, but maybe it was just my paranoia.

A bowl of meth sat on the crusty counter, but no sign of Jackie Daytona. This question was answered in the living room, where meth-fueled bikers blew smoke in my face. Prison would almost be a relief, if I was allowed to cap these fuckboys first. Jackie, looking like one of the royal cards in Alice's Wonderland, demanded some dirtbag "get down on the ground and give him twenty-two." Of course the jackoff was doing it, maybe to get access to the meth bowl.

The room was just crammed with half-naked club whores hanging from doorjambs or decrepit bookcases. Society's Baggers, all weighted down with Buck knives and pistols, practiced their redwings techniques on these slimy pass-arounds, not seeming to notice if they kneeled in piles of dogshit. The women moaned in between drags from their cigarettes. My eyes already burned. If I didn't want to waste any more nightmarish days watching these people flop like beached fish, I had to make my move.

In the middle of this crapfest, Marcel awaited. She posed, hand on hip, on a stool atop a coffee table. Now that she wore a low-cut V-neck dress, I could guess she was really a woman. Her boobs didn't have that artificial balloon look, like nuclear reactors. Tonight the curls of her wig rolled like Disney mermaid hair down over her bare back. Several morons, including Needle-dick Nick and Gangbang Greg, already drooled up at her from their chairs as they fondled their crotches. *Waiting to lick a bleeding lesbian!*

Then I remembered *I* would be expected to do that, and I sidled up to Marcel.

"Remember me?"

She looked me up and down salaciously. "Remember *you*? Who could forget you? You look like a surfer boy from LA."

In spite of myself, I was flattered. "Look, are you really, uh . . . "

"Really bleeding?" she whispered.

"Yes."

"I'll tell only you. No. I'm not. So you can get in line, bum-driller."

Bum-driller? Did everyone on the face of the planet know I was gay?

Heartened by her monthly news, I retreated to the back of the room near the hallway, where Crosley Shelvador was shoving his way to the forefront.

He exhaled his gulp of Budweiser onto my neck. "*Ah. There you are. And there's our lady of the hour.*"

Should I tell him her news? Nah. "You gonna be first in line?"

"I think that honor should go to our man, Tyrone."

"You gonna be second?"

"That's for damned sure."

"Can't wait to, uh . . . ?"

Three more gulps of bad beer. "Lick some pussy," he declared, a singsong goofball.

I finally turned to him. "Have you ever done it?"

"Nope."

"Well," I said, looking him up and down. "The first time might as well be bloody, right?"

"Right!" His smile was almost demonic. What a strange guy.

But when the time came, it seemed that Tyrone would hand the baton to someone else.

"Ladies and germs!" he yelled. He'd now added an unlit cigar to his WWII costume, and he clenched it in his teeth like Groucho. "Welcome to the annual red wings night at the infamous Society's Bag retreat! Tonight the lovely Marina—"

"Marcel," Jackie Daytona reminded him. Jackie stood behind Tyrone, hands clasped behind his back, practically rocking from heel to toe in his excitement. He appeared like a Regency gentleman with his sideburns and platinum curls falling over his forehead. He boasted that sort of snobby, my-shit-don't-stink grin. But even from this distance, his curls quivered with the force of his rapid heartbeat. I had seen guys die from heart attacks when on meth in Hank's Hot Springs. One guy had a stroke, rendered a paralyzed zombie.

Tyrone glanced at Jackie, but said even louder, "*Marina* has offered to be the object of our worship."

"Yeah. Yeah!" goofed Squee. He looked like a buck-toothed kid with his backward baseball cap.

Tyrone blared, "I have kindly stepped aside tonight out of the graciousness of my heart. I am giving the honor to my

Sergeant-at-Arms, Mr. Jackie Daytona. Jackie has been having a rough time of it lately." He formed a fist and punched himself in the chest, near his Filthy Few patch. He might as well have twenty of them. "My heart goes out to you, Jackie, my man. Let's hope we get some relief for you soon."

Jackie bowed his head like some damned servant. I reckoned I could smoke Jackie while he ate out Marcel, and cap Tyrone with practically the same bullet as he stood proudly by. I could be out the front door before anyone realized what was happening. That was how I rocked.

But events of the next few minutes were all up in my shit.

Jackie swaggered over to Marcel, lower jaw jutting with pride. Members cheered and urged him on.

"Eat her!"

"Eat her raw!"

"Raw, raw, raw!"

"That's the spirit we have here!"

With a flourish of the arm, Jackie reached for the hem of Marcel's dress. Perched on her stool, she spread her legs to welcome him in. She leaned back on her hands so her tits protruded. I frowned a little. She seemed to have no nipples underneath the flimsy polyester of her dress.

Jackie bowed again, this time to bring his face to Marcel's crotch level. With a devilish grin, he lifted the skirt, turned his head to her, and dove in.

Oh my saints.

Jackie dove in, only to have a cock slap him upside the head.

"Whoa!"

"Holy shit!"

"What's *that*?"

"Marcel! Are you a boy?"

But no one left the room. Jackie was nonplussed for all of a split second before he regained his composure. He grabbed the naked cock by the base and gulped the whole thing down.

I declare. The way Jackie enthusiastically sucked, his cheeks hollowing out as he even fondled the bulging pair of balls, struck me in a way like no other.

These fucking Society's Baggers. These scumsucking homophobics were fucking hypocrites of the worst order.

"Oh, *yeah*!" yelled Tyrone, fondling his bulging crotch. "Suck that gay dick, Jackie! Suck it!"

Everyone started chanting "Suck it!" I declare, maybe two men left the room gagging. But even Squee, Needle-dick, and Gangbang Greg were standing with gripped fists howling at the moon. Needle-dick had gotten YouTube on his phone, blaring the Beatles' *Polythene Pam*. That was witty as heck. I swear, it was one big orgy in there with the members putting even more *oomph* into licking sweetbutts' twats, and then there was Jackie Daytona.

He was fixing to gulp that entire wang down his throat, that's how much passion and frenzy he put into it.

My body vibrated with anger like a tuning fork. *How dare they.* They tortured and tormented gays every second they were awake, yet "on a dare" they would roar like a bar in Sturgis to congratulate a cocksucker. When Tyrone approached Marcel and reached to grip her balls into a tight sack, that's when I gained the final push over the edge.

I clasped my .45 and tore it from my waistband. Gripping it in a modified Weaver stance—because I had no room to set my feet shoulder width apart—I aimed true at the back of Jackie's heart.

Crosley, who up 'til now had been moaning shit like, "Oh God, Oh God," and "This 'taint right," now bellowed, "*Whoa!* What's this? There's a *shooter* in the room?" while backing off with hands held high.

What the actual fuck? Crosley was throwing me under the bus? I was so shocked all the tension went out of my perfect stance, and I dropped my gun hand to my side.

Funny thing was, no matter how high Crosley shrieked, *no one turned to look at us.* No one, that is, aside from Tyrone

Shoelaces. He dropped his handful of testicles just as fast as I'd dropped my pistol hand, and he looked me straight in the face, open-mouthed.

I ran.

Stumbling after me, Crosley tried to grab my arm but failed. He shout-whispered, "I'll keep your secret if you introduce me to the Zealots!"

Shoving guys aside like they were bowling pins, I ran for the front door, leaping over the supine PJ like I was kicking up my heels in some psoriasis commercial. Still gripping the pistol, my arms pumped almost as athletically as they had when I chased the cat with Hunt.

I jumped on my seat so hard my own balls stung, and by the time I jammed the key into the ignition and drove the pistol into my waistband, Tyrone was hot on my heels. I pulled the choke and squeezed the clutch, as the Prez already huffed and puffed down the dead lawn.

"You fucktard!" he bellowed, raising his clenched fist that had formerly fondled balls. "I'm not gonna let God do the accounting on this!"

As I roared away, I had a free hand to flip him off. "I'm going to tie your tiny dick into a pretzel, you fat asscrack!" I boomed.

In my rearview I saw him in the middle of the street with arms flailing about before he remembered to pull his own Glock. By the time he squeezed the trigger, I was around the corner. It sounded like he shot a neighbor's car.

For the next two hours, I listened to my heart thud.

God, I hate going to bed at night. I always feel so alone.

CHAPTER NINE

Hunt

"So tell us why you want to join the Bent Zealots."

This Prez cut right to the chase.

Yet I was smooth. I had years of experience explaining to people how to use gravitational lensing to look at black hole systems. I could certainly explain why I wanted to toss aside my family and join the closed—and homosexual—society of the Bent Zealots.

I looked fondly at my sponsor Fremont, one of several men sitting around the table in their Happy Hour clubhouse. We weren't in the church, or chapel, room because I wasn't even a Prospect yet. They weren't allowed into church either. "I've known and worked closely with Fremont for years, so I've gotten an overall impression of the club. If you take in a good man like Fremont Zuckerman, then you're all right in my books. He's pert near my idea of the perfect man all around, with his geology, interest in science, plainspoken good-naturedness . . . desire to uplift those around him." Fremont had done a lot of volunteer work with the Navajo down in Father Noel's parish. The government had dumped a shit ton of uranium on them during World War II, and had conveniently only cleaned up the white parts outside their boundaries.

A general wave of grins overcame the badass bikers.

Yet Turk Blackburn had many other questions. "Did you get the job at that missile range nearby? Got to tell you, I'm just weary of these indigent dudes hanging around thinking they can ride off our largesse."

I nodded. "I got it. I figured if I can rent a house here in Rough and Ready it's not an insurmountable commute. And the hours are flex. Right now I'm staying with Fremont here." I grinned.

"Yeah," agreed Fremont, my new roommate and sponsor. "He's very helpful doing dishes."

Lock said, "That'll come in handy when you become a Prospect. But right now we just need you to be a hang-around, to prove your worth."

"I can do that," I said. "My mother imbued me with the concept that men and women are equal, that men need to do dishes too. So I suppose I'm handy around the house. And don't forget. I was married for well-nigh twenty years. Take out trash, pick up eggs, mow lawn, fuck wife."

"In that order," laughed Fremont. He'd been married in the olden days, too.

The heroin addict Rover goofed, "Your job must pay a lot. A doctor and all." He was really hopped up on the idea I was a doctor. Hopefully he didn't have a goiter he needed working on.

I shrugged. "I can rent one of these spectacular mid-century houses you guys favor."

Turk leaned on an elbow. Everyone sort of inclined themselves toward him, prepared for something confidential.

He said, "I just want to know you're serious about your queerness going forward. I've never lost a member back into the outside world, and I'm not about to start."

Steepling my fingers, I leaned forward on my elbows too. Men craned their necks even farther to hear my words.

I was not afraid to play the Appalachia card. "I know I'm not your average biker. I'm pert near the opposite with my jewelry and my 'rock star looks.' I'm learned like your Dr. Moog and this geologist here with his master's from MIT, so I presume you take in all kinds. But I'll tell you. I've known since a teenager I was gay. In the newspaper, Billy Graham railed about renouncing homosexuality next to the *Funky Winkerbean* comic strip. I started believing conspiracy theories. I trusted my friends when they insisted Hillary Clinton had some kiddie porn op in a pizza parlor. I hung out with guys preparing for Armageddon."

Lock and Rover in particular nodded in acknowledgement.

"So I got out. I knew I never fit in with them, and I had an overriding fear of being labeled a faggot. I educated myself. I knew in Princeton I could let my freak flag fly. Which I did, for maybe a year until I met my wife. And I came out to her first this year. I needed to handle the crazy. Fremont here knows that whole shitshow story."

Fremont chuckled. We were the only two guys at the table not drinking beer—even his priestly husband sipped from a glass mug. And of course, some guy in the back of the bar toked weed. But I fit in with these leather vested guys. I knew it in my deepest molecules. Fremont said, "Yeah, his wife was amazingly understanding."

Lock said, "Might have something to do with her coming after the eggs and the lawn."

Everyone laughed, including me. "Yeah, I don't think it was a big reveal for her. I'll tell you this. I've had to question and resolve my doubts, the dark clouds of illusion that I was ever anything but gay. That I'm straight is loonier than me walking a hundred miles without legs."

"Hear, hear," said Turk. "I belonged to a straight MC until I turned thirty, the Bare Bones. I thought I was fooling everyone until the day I came out. They all just nodded like they knew it all along."

I said, "Yes. My best friend at the bomb range said he knew it."

Fremont frowned. "Then proceeded to write you out of his life."

Everyone murmured in anger. Rover even cried out, "Fuck that!" Everyone agreed, "fuck that," and Rover added, "Hey, I'm going to Sailor Jack's jackoff club later today if you want to come."

I was taken aback. Fremont had mentioned Sailor Jack's, describing it as being for "men with a desire for dick play."

I craved dick play more than hot jizz on my face, but I was certain I didn't want to do it with Rover. Fortunately or not, I was saved from responding when the front door opened, letting in a chunk of sun that blinded us. The space filled with an enormous bull of a man, shoulders wide like the Pacific Ocean. When he strode forward and my eyes adjusted, I saw it was Royal, Berkeley's partner.

I half-stood to greet him. Then I saw Van.

He tore off his black skullcap and walked in wringing it, imbued with more trepidation than I'd ever seen in him. Royal stood off to the side as though presenting Van to us. And indeed that's what he was doing.

"Sorry for busting in like this," said the former WWE wrestler, who looked as though he'd like a skullcap to wring. Still a Prospect, Royal liked to wear his cut while shirtless, pleasing everybody. "Looks like you're having a meeting."

"Not really—" I started to say, but Lock cut me off.

"Van?" he said, rising to a stand. "Is that you?"

"Sure is," said my Scots-Irish dream man, stepping forward timidly.

Of course he didn't wear his Society's Bag cut, but he looked . . . different. He lacked that arrogance I'd seen in him, that abundance of pride. It seemed he came forward to a king to ask a lifesaving favor. He disparaged himself, and I wanted to tell him to stop.

"Well," said Lock, "what do you want?"

Van came into the fluorescent light that flooded us all. The scene resembled those dogs playing poker—or the Last Supper, the holy light saturating us, and Lock most of all. His cut was weighted down with patches, in particular the Filthy Few that denoted he'd killed a man.

Van looked about to cry. "I . . . . I'd like to join the Bent Zealots."

Royal added, "I'll sponsor him."

Differing cries rang out. Rover yelled, "No fucking way!" while slapping his thigh. Others just went "whoa," and looked around at each other. I alone remained silent, my eyes drinking in Van's stiff nipples under his plain, tight T-shirt. His casually adjusted his full crotch in the faded 501s, accustomed to nestling his long, thick prick, an outline had been painted into the fabric.

Turk stood too. "Now, now," he admonished us, like we were kids. "We told Hunt here that we already have two Prospects, Berkeley and Royal. Besides, Royal, you can't be a sponsor because you're still a lowly Prospect."

It's safe to say that everyone was shocked when Noel stood. "I'll sponsor him," said the gorgeous, long-haired priest. I'd never get used to seeing him in his garb, even though the clergy shirt's short sleeves gave an informal look under his patched cut. The tab displayed the white clerical collar. Noel was a fulltime Episcopalian priest who adhered to their rules while gracing the motorcycle club immensely with his fatherly presence.

Van came closer to our table. "Really, Father Moloney? I only met you once at the fish fry."

"Yes, but I can tell you're a solid, good man. Just raising yourself out of that holler was a miracle."

"A plum miracle," I agreed.

Noel said, "Like Hunt here. You guys are tarred with the same brush."

Rover declared, "You should *both* come with me to the jackoff club!"

Fremont intervened. "Hey. We're sponsoring them. They're coming with us to get the full picture, not just the one where you get jacked in front of ten men."

A desire for dick play. I would come in my pants if even one knob jockey jacked Van in front of me.

Now Lock waved us away. "All right, all right. I've got to go draw a bead on a guy who broke out of his own courtroom and vanished." Lock owned Los Toros Hermanos Bail Bonds.

"He killed his mother with a hammer to the skull, took a knife and swished her brains around to make sure she was dead, then raped her."

"Godspeed," I said instantly, as did everyone else. I couldn't believe he wasted time on me when he had to deal with that. But one of the tenets of the club was "If you're not living on the edge, you're taking up too much room." The club always came first. *Live to Ride. Ride to Live. I'd better go buy a Harley soon.* My electric I-PACE Jaguar impressed no one.

As we all broke up, Fremont clapped me on the shoulder. "Aren't you two familiar with each other?" He said this loud enough for Van, who was being herded outside by Royal, to hear. Van perked up, refusing to be herded. I had no idea if Fremont had seen us ardently making out by Turk's fence, and I had to have the correct answer.

"Yes. We met at the fish fry."

Rover soon made our status clear. "You'd just met? Man, I was certain you'd been to a jackoff club before. That way you squirted on the cactus was unbelievable, man. Never seen a guy shoot so far. That's why I wanna see it again."

Van and I looked at each other with dismay. Of all the fucking Zealots who could've watched us perform in the desert that day, it had to be fucking Rover.

Father Noel came to our aid. "That's their own damned business, Mr. Florkowski. Come on, let Lock out. You're clogging the doorway."

It might've been our own damned business but my weakened heart thudded with shock to have our intimate activities blared to the club like that. As we shuffled out the front door, I couldn't even look at Van. I just wasn't used to this shit.

However, Van touched my arm. "Hey. Don't pay attention to that smack addict. I'm not ashamed of anything we did."

Royal handed Van a folded square of black leather. "Don't forget about this."

"Oh, yeah," said Van. He searched the little crowd standing in front of the neon sign, *The Happy Hour.* It wasn't hard to sight Father Noel, standing just as tall as the two of us at six foot two. Van threaded his way past a couple bikers and handed Noel the cut that had part of a Society's Bag patch showing. "Here. I'd like to offer this to you guys as a sign of my dedication."

Noel seemed charmed with the gesture. He shook the cut out so we could view the entire disgusting patch as well as the PROSPECT colors. "You're out of the club?" he asked Van.

"Out bad," Van agreed.

Noel folded up the cut again. "Well, that's a start anyway."

Van continued, "And I have to tell you. These Baggers plan to jump you guys at the Kingman run next month. To take *your* colors."

Noel's mouth was a thin line. "Well. Thanks for the heads up. I'm thinking we could use this cut as a decoy. Infiltrate their perimeters."

Van chuckled. "I could only do it by wearing a Mandalorian head, because those jagweeds are fixin' to smoke me. I'll explain later."

Fremont looked at him sideways. "You'd better."

"Meanwhile," said Noel on a fresh tack, "why don't we have a sojourn to Sailor Jack's? Dr. Mountjoy, you up for it?"

A strange way to put it, but I had to smile. I was bold, unafraid to go places.

And if I couldn't do it myself, watching a stranger jack off my Van would be the highlight of my year.

CHAPTER TEN

Van

As I rode to the jackoff club in Hunt's electric Jaguar—Fremont and Noel had insisted we drive together—I couldn't identify my overbearing feeling. It took me a full half hour to figure it out, my fingers strumming the console between us. I was *nervous*. It had been years since I'd been shuddering with anxiety, maybe back when I was first trying to lure the gay out of Claude, to get him to admit he liked me. Once his lust was obvious, we just proceeded in a plainspoken way, not afeared of the other's reactions.

Now? I'd jacked Dr. Mountjoy *once* in an act that was starting to look more like a concerted attack. Damnation, I'd *fallen* upon the poor man and had impressed my will upon him. He didn't have a choice! Sure, he could've fought back or run, especially when I'd kissed him by the fence with Rover and others looking on slack-jawed. Hunt had returned the kiss with ardor, but could that've been because he was taken by surprise? Because I gave him no option? I'd well nigh assaulted the poor astrophysicist, and he might've felt he had no option.

He asked, "You've never been to a jackoff club?"

I shook my head. "Nope. We heard about something like it in Laurinburg, but we got to the doors and changed our mind."

"Why?"

Antsy, I felt for imaginary things in my jean pocket. The fake outdoorsy new leather scent of his car seats was making me ill. "I don't know. Made us skittish thinking of one of us doing something with a stranger. Like . . . we might get jealous or something, I don't know."

Hunt nodded. "I can see that. Are you going to do something with a stranger tonight?"

I knew that question was coming. But what choice did I have? Either I did something with a stranger, or I did something with Hunt. I tried to sound casual. "Sure. Why not? That's the best way to find out about these things."

There was a brief silence. Hunt said, "I wonder if Fremont and Noel do it with other people."

I frowned. "I doubt it. From what I hear, most guys just sit around jacking themselves. Like 'yes' means 'yes' and 'no thank you' really does mean 'no thank you.' There's no blowing or butt play involved. Strictly knob jobs." I was seriously dejected there was no sucking involved. I'd been fantasizing about gorging myself on Hunt's heft since day one. I'd have to find a way to maintain control while pleasuring him. *I* was the top, the Dom. If Hunt went cock-happy at the club squeezing every dong he saw, I'd have to take him into hand. So to speak.

He tossed his beautiful head of lush curls. "I understand if you don't want to go to a club." He just laid that out there for me to pick up on. It was my choice. I liked that. He was easygoing.

"Oh, no. I'm not afeared of any club. Especially not in Yuma, Arizona." I don't really know why Yuma, another bastion of conservative movements, should not fear me in particular. But Sailor Jack's held their Sunday afternoon jerkoff club in this loft space, no sign, nothing to draw attention to it.

In fact, we had to act like toolbags and text Fremont in order to confirm the address. Standing around in front of a jackoff club, practically whistling like jagweeds. Luckily the doorman—we were warned his name was Achilles—came to get us. Up a flight of stairs, he had us sign something that was also printed on a wall sign: "Jack's events may have nudity and solo, mutual, and group exploration of safe sex. No oral or anal contact of any kind!"

"Hunt here is a baby gay," I told Achilles, embarrassing my poor love no end. Hunt looked at the floor and shook his head, almost like he thought *tsk, tsk.*

Handing us numbered knapsacks for our clothes, Achilles said smoothly, "This is the perfect place for newbies to explore. Do nothing but watch — a perfect sanctuary for voyeurs. Men can explore their desire for penis interaction. A place for men to see and be seen."

Penis interaction made my mouth water. I elbowed Hunt, not really sure why. Certainly no voyeur, if anything, Hunt was an exhibitionist, displaying his big dick in the middle of the burning red desert like that. Fact, it was difficult to tell if he was a sub or bottom at all. He'd allowed me to jack him, but in a very powerful, potent, almost aggressive way. I hated to admit it, but Hunt had *me* in the palm of his hand that entire time.

We entered a locker room to disrobe. Confident in my own cut body, I practically whistled as I whipped my clothing off — not that I had much to begin with, feeling nude already with no cut. I flicked my eyes to Hunt a few times, and he was definitely less casual. I had no idea why he wasn't more confident, his pecs shimmering and juicy, abs totally shredded, biceps popping so mightily the veins were the shade of a summer storm. But he wasn't overdone. I hated those gym bunnies who looked as though they were photoshopped. Those biceps literally popped, and scared me. No, Hunt had the perfect balance of muscle versus fat. His beauty showed in his long legs and arms, how he loped like a wolf.

He said, "We haven't seen Fremont and Noel." His broad back to me, I admired the slope of his spine, the salacious jut of his hip bones. He took his time folding his rock star threads into his knapsack.

"They're probably already out there," I said with reassurance. I even put a hand on his shoulder, surprisingly hot and velvety.

He jumped a little. His smile looked forced. "Yeah."

I led the way when we left the room stripped down to our boxer briefs. I wanted to take his hand but didn't dare. We'd held hands after our molestation behind the fish fry, but Hunt didn't even seem that confident now. We entered a large room with a couch and many chairs covered with linen. Pedestal tables held bottles of lube. The spectacle of the men held us awestruck.

Fremont and Noel sat in opposing ottomans stark naked, clutching each other's big dicks. I had to watch Hunt's reaction to see his army airfield friend in this attitude, Fremont's eyes fixed to his lover's, a couple drops of precome shining on his cockhead. I gazed at Dr. Mountjoy's crotch, where his engorged penis strained against the thin cotton, impressing a shadow of his own dickhead there. Damnation, how I wanted to clutch that hard-on, but I wanted to also build suspense — drive my stunning archangel insane with lust, unable to restrain himself.

A wide variety of men reposed in different places, some naked, some less bold in their skivvies. A built Asian guy in his forties with exotic ink decorating his back hand-fucked a tall twenty-something Latino. I was particularly interested in a buff Middle Eastern dude who brought to mind a harem master, his glossy thick locks in a man bun. He made eyes at a Daddy in his seventies. Clad in nothing but a leather harness, the Daddy leaped right to it, palming his son's dick, dry humping his hip, and sliding his tongue down his throat.

My own dick strained my briefs.

I was plumb torn with indecision — interact with another dick, or with my beautiful baby gay? My skittishness became moot when a big-dicked blond college kid lunged for Hunt. I reckon something in Hunt's eyes told the guy to go for it, because the punk right away took a handful of Hunt's erection, squeezing and molding like it was Play-doh. His stupid handsome face was right up against Hunt's — rather, looking up into his eyes with adoration. Was Hunt some kind of daddy too? At thirty-eight and six years older than me, he sported not one grey hair or wrinkle to his face. Yet I'd taken note from Plugr that the term "daddy" had evolved into different realms. There were silver daddies, big daddies, muscle daddies. This guy was definitely worshiping at Hunt's shrine.

I stood lamely with hands at my sides while this football player massaged Hunt's penis, already so stiff his elastic waistband pulled away from his skin.

Even more annoying, Achilles got right up behind me and spoke like a suave, whispering golf announcer. "The mood at J.O. clubs are targeted on physical bliss, the penis in particular. This club is dominated by cocksmen, cock worshipers. This intensely forceful dynamic is due to our displaying what normally is secret, freely sharing it. The practice of our masturbation."

Masturbation my fucking redneck ass. This asshole squiggled his body against Hunt's while corkscrewing his paw around my love's enormous dick—*and he hadn't even taken it into the open yet.* Hunt's features were difficult to read. His eyelids drooped, his lower lip glistened with spit, and he thrust his crotch forward a bit, hands on hips.

Okay, I guess that wasn't too hard to read. He wanted this college kid to jack him.

I tried to sound casual over the low EDM music as I tossed over my shoulder, "So no emotions come into play here?"

Achilles said, "We try not to involve drama. We have wristbands available that can say 'please don't touch' for men who are solely voyeurs."

"Or exhibitionists," I added, as the kid finally yanked Hunt's drawers down.

Is Hunt an exhibitionist? I thought of Turk's backyard, when Hunt's fat cock spurted jizz on the cactus. He didn't give a toss who was watching. *Neither did I.*

His enormous dick bobbed heavily in the lavender-scented air, and he bit his lower lip. Already a few other men gathered around, admiring the Scots-Irish newcomer. I understood a lot of them were allegedly straight, bicurious men, not unlike my man himself. It figured these men would crowd around Dr. Mountjoy as he reveled in "penis exploration."

No one crowded *me*, although my dick was just as hard, long, and thick.

Maybe their bicurious antennae had picked up on Hunt's baby gayness.

Yeah, that was it. At least, that's what I told myself.

Someone loudly squirted a jet of lube onto Hunt's dick so the kid could slide his fist up and down. Hunt sucked in air when the fist glided over his tight glans. I nearly jumped when the leather Daddy several yards away cried "Ah!" My eyes automatically darted to him just in time as he blew his wad on the kneeling, Arabic guy's face. The "son" opened and closed his mouth like a suckling baby to taste some jizz and to simultaneously feel some splash on his cheek. It was a performance piece, pure and simple. *What I wouldn't give to be doing that.*

It give me an idea. When the Daddy dismissed the Bedouin curtly to go wipe off his dick, I stalked over to the kneeling guy. Hands on hips, I nodded down at him as he ran his forearm across his face. A beautiful man with a wide open face, his dark eyes just drank me in. Well, my erection. I nearly wielded it over his forehead.

He nodded back.

As the glossy-haired man took my hard dick out, I couldn't resist glancing at Hunt. The stupid college kid jacked him slowly while about four men now oohed and aahed, fondling their own packages. I feared Hunt would get used to this adulation and start playing the field. My heart thudded, jiggling my Celtic cross pendant lying on my pectoral. I had to hurry this guy up and steal the show, so I stroked the back of his head. There was no oral play involved here, unfortunately, so I couldn't just jam it into this guy's talented mouth, making it a tournament with Hunt.

"Jack me," I encouraged. "Jack me fast."

"Oh." His smile curved his face. He even had a Middle Eastern accent. "You want wham bam thank you ma'am."

"That's it."

Hunt saw me now, and his jaw dropped even lower. He'd never seen my naked dick, and I proudly jutted it into this guy's hand. I gained a couple of self-pleasuring admirers, even one who came over to me from Hunt. They urged my son to "jack that dick" and "make him come all over your face." Except, I think in their jargon they were begging him to make me cum.

Even with seven men gathered around him, Hunt craned his neck to observe me. He made no bones about wanting to see my penis, and my puffing ego pumped my dong even farther, stretching it to unheard-of proportions in my son's fist. Whereas Hunt's admirer was taking his time, drooling all over the beautiful appendage, a plethora of naked dickheads decorating his blond head like a crown, my dark lover jacked me like greased lightning, his fist a blur.

"Oh yeah oh yeah oh yeah," I found myself grunting. The familiar desire raced up the skin, the underside of my prick as I thrust into his palm. My ballsac tightened up against my body, filled with seed. I saw Hunt's ballsac equally as tight under the ministration of his jock, but I was going to be the winner of this race. I was going to jizz all over this gorgeous Arabian face, releasing my load onto his hairless chest, my thick gooey streams—

"*Enough.*"

When Hunt butted his hand against the jock's shoulder, detaching the guy from my penis, I was very surprised. I really was.

I tried hard to be mad, but it was difficult. "What're you doing?"

"Yeah!" said my slave. "What're you doing? I had him *this close—*"

Hunt jutted his lower jaw. "Never mind. Bugger off. This is my man."

The guy's mouth drooped. "Is that true?" he asked me, seemingly very surprised.

I looked Hunt right in the eye. It was easy since we were both the two tallest men in the room. He seemed angry, as his nostrils flared with a rapid breath. Our bare erections bobbed against each other, tightening my balls even higher.

But his eyes never wavered. Leisure and serenity, the watchwords at Sailor's Jacks, had gone right out the window. Some of the men around us even stopped jacking themselves, eager to see how this played out.

At last I said through clenched teeth, "*Your* man?"

"You heard me."

"Okay." I complied. "If I'm your man, then you're going to beat me off, using both your damned hands."

Some unseen guy was at the ready, spritzing gel onto my dick, without touching it for fear of Hunt's ire. I'd never seen my archangel this pissed off. His dick never waned as he grabbed mine in one possessive grip. His other clapped my balls and squeezed at just the right tension, tightening my nipples, making my asshole clench. We still locked each other with our gazes, but as he pumped me I knew a few drops of precome spurted from my tip. Hunt seemed to know it too, as he swiped his thumb over my corona.

I knew my eyelids fluttered and a slight gasp escaped me. He'd know he had me in the palm of his hand.

I had to regain dominance. "You ever had a real lover before? At college maybe?"

"No," he said, almost angrily. "Just some fag who taught me about dicks."

"What was your favorite part?"

Hunt didn't hesitate. "Pleasuring him. If that meant he jacked or sucked me, that was his pleasure. But I loved making him jizz too."

"So he was your real lover."

"No. He never mentioned it, and we weren't seen in public. You and I are seen in public." He swiped his ball fingers across my perineum, just barely rimming my puckered hole. I gasped again, and squeezed my eyes shut. For a sub, he was sure being dominating. He seemed not to notice the circle jerk of men surrounding us, urging us on.

"That's it. Jack him."

"That's your lover? You're one damned lucky man."

"I want to see him shoot all over the dark one."

I supposed Hunt was "the dark one" with his abundance of espresso locks. He corkscrewed his hand obscenely around my dick, and I threaded my fingers together at the base of my skull so I could swivel and rotate my hips. My performance was strictly for Hunt, and I imagined by the melting of his irises that he was falling for me in this act. Some guy on his knees tried to dust my cock with kisses, but Achilles grabbed him and tossed him aside, reminding him of the rules. It cast the scene even more lewdly, that only Hunt was allowed to bring me to orgasm.

I ventured, "So we're real lovers?"

Right when I uttered "lovers," I lost it. Hunt diddled my hole with his fingertip and expertly jacked me, and I just lost my load. He had me angled so high the first shot hit him in the chin, then his pecs sprinkled with feathery, fine hair.

He finally grinned. "That's it, Van. Give it all to me. You're mine, and mine alone. You're my boy from the holler, ain't you? What a fucking hot load you've got for me. That's it. Let it all go. You're with me now."

And I guessed I was.

When it finally ended—with a giant flourish I might add, spurting right onto his exquisite four-pack—I clutched Hunt's buff shoulders, my tense breath stuttering while my eyes rolled into my skull.

He had every right to laugh at me, but he didn't. In fact, his slack jaw told me he was in awe of me. He made no move to wipe my jism from his torso. Fact, he mushed his carved chest to mine and muttered against my mouth, "Van Rossi. My man."

And he kissed me deeply, like we had on the cliff behind Turk's. He slid his warm tongue against my upper palate, and I swirled mine beneath his. We feasted on each other as though in love, and some perceptive jackoff nearby gushed,

"Oh, man! These two are really meant for each other."

It wasn't until much later I realized it was Father Noel, Fremont's partner.

Maybe that's what set me off. But now I had a mind to regain control of the scene. Withdrawing from Hunt with a loud smack, I grabbed a handful of his luscious hair and growled, "You. Turn around."

He did as commanded, and I plastered my moist pubic mound to his meaty ass. His chance now to slither his fingers behind his head, around my neck, twining them together. He ground his haunches against me erotically, jamming my half-mast cock against his crease.

I demanded, "Someone, some lube."

The blonde college kid complied, and a bolt of jealousy stabbed my stomach. However, Achilles ensured the jock didn't linger too long smearing his cock, and I batted away his greedy hand.

I muttered into Hunt's ear as I twisted my fist around his prick, "You've been wanting this, Hunt. Ever since I jacked you in that desert, you've been fantasizing about this."

"Oh, yeah," he agreed, voice heavy with lust.

I sucked on the rim of his ear. "But now you've got fifteen horny guys aching for you. Look at that daddy. He just came, but he's already hot for you. Look, my Arabic guy doesn't even want the daddy anymore. He's just drooling for you."

Like a true scientist, Hunt acknowledged the facts. "He wants me to come on his face."

That angered me. I jacked him harder and faster, like I had behind Turk's house. However, that time there weren't ten eager mouths waiting to taste his spunk. "You wanted your own blond little son to masturbate you, like any good daddy."

"Yes, I did," he admitted breathlessly.

"You forgot you had a man. Me."

"Yes. You."

"You don't think there's someone else eager to taste your jizz? How about me, Van Rossi? I've been dying to taste it since I first laid eyes on you—at the fish fry," I felt compelled to add. My dick was already plumping up again as I dry humped him, squishy between his ass cheeks. Achilles cut us some slack since we were the main draw at the moment, I supposed.

However, other guys, some kneeling, were uttering shit like,

"*I* want to taste that cum."

"Splash it on me, big daddy."

"Feed me your cock."

Bless their hearts, they all wanted a piece of *my man*, and I wouldn't let them have it. When I felt Hunt's cockhead strained beyond belief, I quickly dropped to my knees, elbowing aside the jock and the harem guy.

"Come on come on come on come on," I muttered, as Hunt dug his fingers into my shoulders.

The explosive release was quick. As he jerked his hips spasmodically, he splashed me with a gratifying burst of jizz. My face—I quickly licked it from my lips—my throat, my chest. It seemed evident he hadn't come since the desert. A couple of guys ran their hands over my chest, tweaking my nipples, just to get a palmful of the holy semen. I guessed that was all right with Achilles, or he was jacking himself too.

Squirt after squirt decorated my torso until I was dripping with the stuff. And yes, the blond guy did lean in to lap my abs and I didn't mind because it felt so heavenly. I *wanted* Hunt to be admired, and he was the big dog of the tanyard today. "Uhhhh . . . " he heaved as I milked the last drop. It was like being in the desert, except I was the lucky cactus.

Other men were doing a good enough job of it. I did have to swat away a hand that tried to envelope my prick, but I didn't mind the guys massaging Hunt's jizz off me. I pressed out the last delicious drops with my thumb on the underside of his cock, and y'all, I couldn't resist flicking the tip of my tongue against the hole. No one said a word, but Hunt gasped.

I was in love.

I'd suspected as much before, when I only had his computer image to arouse me.

Now I was convinced. Father Noel was right. We *were* created for each other.

I was in love with a man I'd catfished. Another secret I'd take to the great beyond.

In a weird way, I didn't need to mourn Claude anymore. I had much of that back now, the comfort, the intelligent conversations, the ease. *The companionship.* Hunt and I were in somewhat of the same place, both coming out of our closets in a big way. Joining an MC only made the change, the shift in life's parameters, even wilder. We existed now to buoy each other up.

Hunt panted, draped his forearm before his face as though he didn't want to look at the ocean of men jacking themselves, hot for his body. I stood slowly, running my chest up his torso and gently removing the arm from his face. He peeked at me, almost shy. His very slight grin told me he was happy.

"Hey, cumon," I said cheerfully, as though we stood in a grocery store and not a jackoff club. "Pinky's waiting for us back in Rough and Ready. She has a few houses she wants to show you."

"Pinky, the realtor?"

"That one. Royal and Berkeley own some rental houses in the area where we could squat until you find the one you want to buy." I realized that sounded very presumptuous of me, but damn, I wanted to be with him. Maybe the Zealots could pay me to repair their rides. Then I could pay Hunt rent.

"You bastard," Hunt teased, and pressed a big, sloppy kiss on me.

"Hurray," a few men uttered.

I could not agree more.

CHAPTER ELEVEN

Hunt

"I'll tell ya, the one problem with these houses is that if you need to fix the plumbing, you have to jackhammer all this concrete under our feet."

I nodded, taking it all in. Pinky seemed to have become an expert on mid-century houses in the blink of an eye—she'd moved into one, and now showed us another on Sandcastle Court owned by Berkeley and Royal. They didn't bother staging it, assuming I would buy it. The inspector had found some leaky pipes as well as the overhead stovetop fans that needed replacing. No big deal, especially with a handyman like Van around. Technically a welder, he claimed he knew about water pipes.

"No problem," he said. "I'll just borrow a jackhammer from the Zealots, pour fresh concrete when it's done."

Pinky crossed her arms over her stomach. Today she wore a pink short-sleeved sweater under her suspenders. I figured it was her official realtor costume. "What about the floor tiles? When you rip them out, they're gonna be history."

Van shrugged as though it were no big deal. "I'll have to retile this whole hallway and foyer with something appropriate."

Pinky nodded curtly. "I've seen some midcentury-looking tiles at Home Depot." She turned to observe me with a fresh eye. "Well, well. Great Caesar's Ghost. My crew and I used to listen to your CDs. You sound fat when you sing."

"Pinky!" cried Van, shoving her by the arm.

She held her hands out innocently. "What, what? I tells it like I sees it."

Van said, "Well, you're not going to have any clients if you keep doing that. Remember, you said 'to be a big shot you got to act like a big shot.' Hunt, as you can see, is thin and buff. He's a major wolf."

Pinky eyeballed me. "I can see that."

I liked that Van called me a wolf. Wolves, I found out, had a lean, muscular build and were assertive in their desire for sex. I was all of those things, now that I fell into my new role. Van and Fremont had even helped me purchase a brand new Harley Dyna Wide Glide. Van was in the process of installing a set of aftermarket cams with radical profiles for racing, as he said. He'd put in a better carb, bigger sleeves, pistons, and fairings. He seemed to be intent on me racing — or needing to go somewhere fast . . .

As we walked through the living room to the backyard, Pinky asked Van, "It's so odd that you, too, were familiar with Great Caesar's Ghost. Yet you didn't recognize Hunt when you first saw him?"

Van waved her away. "*Aaa*. Didn't recognize him, no. I just heard their music here and there. Too bad you had to break up."

I said, "We had to. There wasn't enough time for studies and music. So you heard us when you were down in the holler?"

Van shrugged as we took seats around the table. He and Pinky grabbed their soda bottles, and I wrapped my hand around a cup of hibiscus tea. "Sure, why not? My friend had an obscure sense of music. We listened to that radio station WACK and that type of thing. Hey, I had talent. I was more of a chemist than a drug dealer. I justified my actions with my own corrupt ethics code. I wasn't a snitch or a kiddie rapist, right?"

"Right," said Pinky. "No one needs a hearty laugh like the really deeply fucked."

"Exactly," said Van.

"Hey, let me take a picture of you guys. My fourth clients in Rough and Ready."

Van and I glanced uncomfortably at each other, each probably for different reasons. I still wasn't fully untroubled by my out gay status, and Van? He was probably still mortified that he came from those gay-bashers, Society's Bag.

Yet we scooted our chairs closer and leaned in. While Pinky thumbed away on her phone, tongue sticking out the corner of her mouth, we talked.

Van said, "Believe it or don't, I earned a half million bucks a year. But I lived in this decrepit trailer. My addiction just ravaged me. Paper money blew around the joint, got sucked into ceiling fans. Guys hung around just to grab the bills that blew into in the street, bless their hearts. My Jaguar—yeah I had a Jag, though not electric like yours—was repo'd. I just dripped sweat, panicking that shadow people were after me."

I tried to be casual about this scenario. "Sounds like Jackie Daytona of the Baggers."

"Oh, ho," barked Pinky. "He *did* see shadow people. You can't know how glad I am I left. I don't mind being alone without my crew. I just don't want to be irrelevant."

Van said, "You got enough pictures, Pinky? I'll tell you the truth, Hunt. I put foil over my windows."

I nodded, glancing at Van's profile. My face softened with fondness. The tawny, rocky hills behind the house reflected warmly on his handsome features.

"I would close my eyes, hoping no one saw me. I heard clobbering at my front door. *Police.* I raced to flush drugs, but I clogged the toilet. Men in blue broke down the bathroom door, but I was out the window. Yep, I went out through the bathroom window."

"Thank God." The story got *me* a bit nervous, and I didn't like when my heart sped up.

"See, I could've been an informant just like Crosley."

"Who's that?" I asked.

Pinky said, "You don't wanna know. An informant pretending to be a Society's Bagger."

Van said, "I didn't tell you. When I was about to pop off Jackie Daytona, Crosley yelled out, 'there's a shooter in the house!' That's what spooked me into not shooting. I thought I was doomed. That fucking cockbite!"

Putting her phone down, Pinky snorted and giggled. "Cockbite. Sounds like Jackie Daytona was the cockbite."

Van had told me he'd been so freaked by the violent antics of the Baggers that he'd been about to put a bullet into the back of Daytona's skull. It was a new way of living for me, and I stretched the boundaries of my psyche to understand. It brought to mind the holler life we'd all thought we'd left behind, only to find out we were smack in the middle of it again. I could understand loathing the hypocritical bikers who slandered us during the daytime, and at night pawed over cocks. He'd told me about Daytona eagerly diving into the crotch he'd assumed was a bloody pussy while the other cockbites egged him on. I wanted desperately to help Van exit that reality.

Maybe deep down, I was still that bad boy from the holler. Maybe after a decade of safe, wholesome family living, I was prepared for danger.

Van said, "This is serious as a heart attack, Pinky. Oh. Sorry, Hunt." He put his hand on my forearm and left it there, shaking his head while regarding me with amazement. I frowned. What did he see that I didn't? "You're a successful, academic, gorgeous, stable man with a beautiful home. I'm an ogre under a bridge."

The sorrow of this statement got to me, and I laid a hand over his. "You left, Van. You got out."

"Yeah, and right back into the fire with the Baggers," Pinky said as she tapped her phone.

Van opened his mouth to snark back, instead leaping to his feet and pointing with a stiff arm. "Cat!"

Pinky and I followed suit, jumping as though electrocuted. My rational brain took control, and I said, "Don't anyone move!"

The Maine Coon had spotted us and went still as a glass lake. Mighty's lime green eyes stood out starkly against fur the shade of an oncoming storm. He was majestic as a panther padding through jungle undergrowth. Tufts of silver fur puffed from the tips of his ears, slightly flattened against his Mighty skull.

Pinky spoke from the corner of her mouth, her hands stretched into claws. "Does anyone have any food he might like?"

Van said, "I have beef jerky in my saddlebags."

I couldn't resist saying, "That has so much sodium."

Van made a quiet lip fart. "It's good enough for luring."

Pinky said, "Mighty seems to like your new house. You said you were leaving cat food behind Berkeley's house?"

I said, "Yeah, but Berkeley doesn't want to. Reminds him of the old days when a hundred decaying cardboard cats were stacked up in his place."

Mighty took one tentative step toward us, and we all hissed in air. Too afraid to believe he might actually approach us, like a stray dog dying to be petted.

But cats weren't like that. Someone must've breathed too hard, for Mighty darted off behind some tiny saguaros with brilliant magenta flowers. He paused long enough for us to gulp air, then scooted off over the low fence toward a craggy rock formation.

We all exhaled. Pinky in particular acted like she'd just walked through a war zone—groaning, smearing her hair back from her forehead, looking despondently at the table. In fact, she picked up her phone. What she saw made her forehead wrinkle and her mouth sneer. "What the . . . " She glanced at me.

What? What about me? But instead of telling me, she said, "Hey, guys. Maybe start luring him from here with the wet food. Use raw hamburger or something. Meantime, go look again at those master bathroom tiles. If they seriously need replacing, we can lowball the owners."

Van said, "Lowball Berkeley and Royal?"

But we didn't protest being ordered to be alone with each other in a tiny enclosed room.

On our way, I said, "I suppose we shouldn't try to lowball our friends. This is their new business they built from scratch."

Van said, "Well, Berkeley still gives painting classes in town. He makes coin. Turk and Rover are his star students."

I nearly choked as we rounded the corner into the hallway. "Seriously? I could maybe see Turk, but *Rover*? What does he paint, nudes?"

Van chuckled. "Apparently he's into some sort of cubism. Whatever that is."

"Well, it gives me hope for the human race." Hands on hips, I studied the shower tiles again. They definitely weren't original. Looked like someone in the eighties had put an eighties idea of what the early sixties were like. "This'll cost about five grand to redo." I knew that, because I'd redone my own master shower at one of my homes with Lauren.

Van didn't seem to want to discuss tiles. He faced me squarely, buff arms crossed before his chest. "Hope is a big discipline, Hunt. It's not passive. It really demands active work."

I turned to him. This didn't sound like my Van the Man hailing from Hank's Hot Springs. "You're getting mighty philosophical."

He shrugged. "I read some Zen. 'More valuable than treasures in a storehouse are the treasures of the body, and the treasures of the heart are most valuable of all.'"

I grinned. "We don't see that the Buddha exists in our own hearts."

His eyebrows raised, as if surprised I knew that. "Yes!" He strutted a bit, there in the echoey empty bathroom. "'Merely seeing each other's face would be insignificant. It's the heart that is important.' You're surprised I read that?"

He sure was placing a lot of importance on the heart, for some raggedy reason. "Not really. *The Writings of Nichiren Daishonen?*"

He latched his fiery eyes onto mine. "Exactly." Taking one stride, his torso was plastered to mine. He spiked his fingers through my hair behind my skull, cradling it in his palm. "God, you make me hot. Honestly, Hunt. Watching those men drool over you at Sailor Jack's earned a permanent place in my hot memory bank. I've jacked off every night thinking about that. That one blond kid who thought you were his daddy."

I scoffed. "I'm hardly old enough."

"How old are your kids?"

"Eighteen and sixteen."

"Then you're a daddy. It made me realize how much you control me. I'm just mud in your hands, Dr. Mountjoy."

He kissed me then as if to shut me up. His pelvis pressed mine up against the vanity while his lips smashed against mine, relaxing into me. He sucked on my lower lip and a thrill shot through my spine. *What does he mean . . . I control him?* I could hardly reason it out with Van massaging my scalp and thrusting his long, fat prick against mine. It made him hot to see me handled . . . to be desired by others . . .

Detaching his mouth with a smack, he muttered, "Pray to the heavenly gods with all your heart."

And with this, he dropped to his knees.

I inhaled sharply with the swift sensation of heat—he pressed his open mouth to my cock and exhaled through the velvet. It was like someone had thrust a cup of hot coffee against me. Van breathed as I clutched his shoulders, and he munched my cockhead through the fabric.

But this was not his full intent. Fingers grabbling against my belt buckle, he swiftly had the buttons undone, my pants and briefs pooling around my knees. He gripped my cock at the base, gazing as though praying.

I murmured with a voice unexpectedly full of love. "'Be ever diligent in your faith, so your desire will be fulfilled.'"

Instead of slurping up my cock, which I assumed was his heart's desire, Van tilted his head back even further, lifted my prick, and sucked in my ballsac.

Damnation. All perception and feeling drained from my own head, and I felt I'd passed out for a fraction of a second. Intensity and ardor swept down into my balls, and my prick bobbed as it squirted precome. Van ducked up and down, lips stretched over teeth, sucking my sac, then releasing it just as fast. He'd lick and lap like it was an art form, then bob back away from me, leaving my sac swinging in the breeze.

I leaned into the rhythm, learning to sway my hips and land my testicles in his hot mouth. Teabagging, I'd heard this called on the hookup sites. It was like dipping your teabag into a hot cup of water, leaving your essence therein. And yes, it was a Dom/sub game, where Van was the submissive.

But how dominant was I really, when Van was the one controlling the bliss? Every time I bent to dip my balls in his hungry mouth, this luscious, talented ghettobilly thrilled me with his mouth, his tongue. I struggled to remain in charge, thrusting my hips against his face to dip my sac against his teeth. Van sipped and lapped as though drawing the semen out of my very scrotum, and each lick of his tongue sent me closer to the very edge of release. *And he wasn't even licking my cock.*

Another burst of precome, and my hand went to my penis. Using the semen at the tip as lube, I gave myself a few quick strokes that sent me to the brink. My moans bounced around the tiled enclosure.

But Van released my balls. Lust dropped quickly away from the precipice. My eyes popped open to see him flat on his back, wiggling his fingers for me.

"Sit on me," he commanded. "Sit on my face."

CHAPTER TWELVE

Van

I knew I was asking for a lot. I was being the same demanding asshole I'd been behind Turk's house when I'd well nigh assaulted this sensitive, sensuous love of mine.

Yet this was somewhat different. I was asking *him* to assault *me*, in a way. He grinned impishly at my suggestion, standing above me with hands on hips, big dong throbbing with his heartbeat. *His heartbeat . . . his heart so delicate . . .*

He unzipped his boots and kicked them off. His velvet pants slithered easily to the floor in a puddle, and he just stepped from them. With one foot on either side of my chest, his cock loomed large.

"Just making sure," he said, "you literally want me to sit on your face."

"Yup," I chirped. "Turn around."

Hunt turned and kneeled, and I ran a hungry hand up that silken, curvy backside.

I smacked him hard with my stiff palm. He gasped and jumped. But he said nothing, so I took that as submission, and I did it again. His fleshy white butt reddened with each slap, so I did it to the left side.

"Yeah," I encouraged. "You like this, don't you?"

He panted. "I don't know. Never had it done to me before."

"You'll soon find out," I said with authority, and did it again. His cock twitched with each spank, and I used my other hand to spread his cheeks apart. Now I could cuff him closer to the virgin asshole, his little pucker just dying for some action. He huffed and gasped with each blow, now bent so low his torso was horizontal as he clung to the toilet. This gave me free rein to slap that swinging ballsac a few times, getting almost playful, like a cat with a toy.

He really groaned now, and I became afraid I was pushing it. So I let up on the spanking and just kneaded and cupped the luscious globes. I tickled the rim of his hole and said, "This daddy is just dying for some tongue."

"How'd you know?" he whispered harshly.

That was all I needed. Plunging my face into his crotch, I lapped at his balls, just as I had while teabagging. But being flipped around this time, my nose was in his hole, and I could flick my tongue all the way up his sensitive perineum to reach it. Zigzagging my tongue this way, I could tease his sac, perineum, and hole all at the same time.

The effect was astounding.

"Oh, *God!*" he yelled, his cry echoing in our tiny chamber. Whenever I flitted my tongue around his pucker his entire body would tense up, and I had the idea to slap his prick. Making smaller and smaller arcs with my tongue, I finally darted the tip in, causing my lover to groan and arch his back. Gripping his fat prick made him clench his ass cheeks, so I kept it up. He clutched that toilet like it was the day after Super Bowl, and he fucked the air to encourage more tongue action.

"You fucking raggedy Tar Heel! How'd you learn to play a man like this? You been around the block with your talented . . . fucking . . . oceanic . . . "

I could tell when his voice lost traction and he uttered "oceanic" — that was the color of my eyes, I'd learned — that he was slipping into orgasm.

I didn't want to lose this chance.

Gripping his hips, I swiveled him so he faced me. Now he collapsed to grab the edge of the bath tub where I'd scooted myself up. He fisted his own bursting cock, jabbing his dripping cockhead at me. "This time," he huffed, "you get to suck my meat."

Just hearing him say that, *suck my meat*, sent me into a frenzy. I grappled for his dick too, thumbing the glistening drip of jizz at the slit. "I owe you a debt of gratitude," I groaned before diving in.

Oh. My. Saints. I *gulped* that penis, I mean *gulped* it. I'd been so starved for it at the club when every last manjack was drooling for it. Because of their numbnuts rules, my only reward had been a squirt in the face, a tantalizing taste of the tart jizz. Some other fools even slurped or wiped the precious elixir from my torso just to get a morsel of it. Now I gulped and slathered my tongue like I was underwater sucking an air hose for life itself. No penis was too big for me as I swallowed and gobbled Dr. Mountjoy's big old horse cock with my eager throat.

Oh Lord, after these weeks of denial, I was ready for a hearty stomach full of his semen.

I was proud of how swiftly he climaxed. He kneeled tall with his head thrown back, one hand glued to the back of my skull, needlessly pressing me to taste more, more, more. He inhaled and held his breath, and I felt the surge of come up the underside of his prick. Because I swallowed him so deeply, it hit the back of my throat, and I had to unhinge my jaws in order to chew and roll the tangy jizz around my mouth, like tasting a fine cab, if I'd ever done such a thing.

It seemed Hunt didn't breathe at all as he shuddered and jutted into my mouth. This lasted a long while with spurt after spurt coating my palate. He was surrendering to another man for the first time, and *that man was me. I* was the chosen one to lick Hunt to ecstasy, and I was proud of it.

Except for the nagging memory at the back of my skull. I had catfished him. How could I ever be a true, honest lover when I was at heart a trailer park all-star, a hilliterate fooling him into sex?

If it wasn't for that, I'd say this was the beginning of true love. I needed, wanted, and craved this man, mayhap on a truer level than I'd craved Claude. This man was my stunning archangel, a hundred times more accomplished, intelligent, and admirable than poor son of the soil, Claude Berger. Poor *dead* Claude.

And I could never say his name to Hunt, or it would inspire furious, unforgivable reminders.

"Ahhhh." Hunt finally breathed and relaxed. His cock still twitched in my mouth, and I spun my tongue around its softening length. He tousled the back of my head, loosening his grip on my skull. When I pulled back enough to look up, Hunt was grinning fondly down on me. *Success.* I had lured him in. "I'm starting to get used to you."

I withdrew his cock with a loud smack. I couldn't resist giving his ballsac a sharp wet slap, although I knew it was painfully exquisite for him. "I don't ever want to be without you, Hunt."

We smiled mindlessly at each other until some commotion came from the house's interior. Some guy had busted in, and was shouting something fierce at Pinky, maybe from the kitchen.

Hunt lurched to his feet, grabbing his puddle of velvet from the floor. I didn't have much to put back on, so after finger-combing my hair in the mirror I placed my ear to the closed door.

"Do you know who it is?" asked Hunt, sitting to zip up his boots.

Un-fucking-fortunately, I did.

Crosley Shelvador was orating at Pinky in a high, distressed voice. "Then Tyrone yelled at me because we were moving a mattress for Squee!" With each syllable, his voice went higher, like one of The Chipmunks.

Pinky barked, her tension obvious. No doubt she was hoping we'd locked the bathroom door. "What's wrong with moving a mattress?"

Crosley was agitated. Just his presence at our new home meant trouble. Why had he fled the Baggers? "Well, we had no rope! So naturally I said I'd lie on top of it on the roof of his cage. It was like parasailing!"

"I'll bet."

"Squee got up to about thirty miles an hour on Stone Free Drive, that's when the fluttering and shaking became super-violent. I kept my grip real good, digging my fingers into the foam rubber. I was shaking like a junkie, like a whore in church!"

"Hey, would you like a warm bottle of water?"

Crosley was carried away with his story by now. "I was screaming at Squee to stop, to slow down, but my voice got ripped away with the wind. Eventually my weight wasn't enough to hold it down and we — well, the mattress and me — went flying over this slot canyon, this seasonal flash flood place."

"Was there water in there?"

"Luckily not. It was actually kind of nice for a few seconds, floating over the rocks, even though I knew I'd crash."

"Wait, what does this have to do with Tyrone Shoelaces?"

I glanced at Hunt, who was buttoning his fly. "I'm going out," I announced, like a battlefield private in a movie. In a way, it was similar. The combination of Pinky and Crosley as they clashed in the center of an empty space was definitely volatile.

Hunt asked, "Who's that guy? You know him?"

I had to think fast, not one of my talents. "That informant I mentioned earlier." How could I avoid saying that? I'd already made note of it, not expecting in a million years Crosley would actually show up anywhere.

I strode down the hallway toward the kitchen. Crosley's voice was as high as the berries on a wild ash tree by now.

"Tyrone shredded me in front of the whole club! He called me a jagov, a coozemonkey, and a skidmark! PJ and Squee were laughing their butts off and I had to sit there and take it!"

Pinky scoffed. "What else is new, Crosley? He called me an assclown while I was serving thirty bikers drinks."

I reached the kitchen. Crosley stood tall, his Society's Bag cut making him a giant target. His arms bent at right angles to his body, elbows close to his hips like he was about to bust out into a Michael Jackson robot dance. Only his hands flapped. "Yeah, but you know how into it Tyrone gets! He was, like, *orating* about my failures in front of everyone. He wouldn't stop! Hey, Van. You can back me up."

I said, "Nope, I wasn't there. I'm out bad, in case you forget. But yeah, Tyrone can be pretty damned harsh. That's one of the reasons I left. Why are you here?"

Crosley splayed his hands out to present me with the facts. "Well, without you the club's a shitshow, mechanically speaking. Jackie Daytona's pickup truck needed new brake pads. I mean what do I fucking know from shinola? I managed to get the old ones out, and there I was, trying to install new ones."

"It's just a few bolts," I said.

"Yeah, *but*. The new ones were thicker and didn't fit—"

I said, "Right, the calipers are self-adjusting. You need to spread them apart."

"What? But we had no jack, so I drove the truck up onto a spare tire so I could lie beneath it."

"Uh-oh," both Pinky and I said in tandem. I added, "I can see where this is going."

Crosley pointed at me. "*Exactly!*" As though he was proud of it. "The truck rolled off the tire onto me, and Jackie Daytona has the nerve to screech at *me*? I'm the one with the broken shinbone!" To demonstrate, Crosley hobbled around the narrow kitchen a bit.

Pinky tried to move things along. "So how does this translate into you being here, Crosley?"

"Well, I lost it, like Van the Man here did! I had my Glock, naturally, so I just pulled it on him."

"On Jackie?" we asked.

"On Jackie! Needle Dick Nick and Gangbang Greg were witnesses! Just like they were to you, Van, when you pulled that piece on Jackie at the red wing party. Except they didn't see you do it. Only Tyrone and me did, and let me tell you, Tyrone is out for blood."

"I know," I said wearily. Hunt came up behind me, his boot heels tromping on the old vinyl tile. Reaching a hand out blindly, I slid my palm down his arm in a comforting manner. I had a feeling he'd need comforting after all this drama. Being a regular family man and all, everything was so new to Hunt. Not so to me. Un-fucking-fortunately I was used to all the bloodshed. "So you pulled your iron but didn't use it?"

"Didn't use it. Like you, I chickened out."

Pinky stepped between us. "Hey. A chicken is the last thing Van the Man here is."

Hunt grinned that starstruck, angelic grin where his eyes actually glittered. "Van the Man," he echoed.

"Well," protested Crosley, "needless to fucking say, I'm out bad too! Now how'm I going to get intel from them to feed my parole officer?"

It was my turn to step up. "Hey, hey. You talk about being an informant enough, you won't *need* a parole officer. You'll need a guardian angel."

Hunt muttered, "Oh, is this the guy . . . ?"

Pinky held her palms to the ceiling. "All right, all right! Crosley, meet Hunt Mountjoy. Hunt, meet Crosley the Nark. And no, Crosley, you're never gonna be accepted into the Bent Zealots with our knowledge of who you are."

"Shit!" I was getting pissed Crosley had transferred his blowback onto us. "It's a miracle enough they might accept *me*—let's not push our fucking luck!"

Crosley seemed to have moved onto a different subject. Narrowing his eyes, *he* stepped up to *Hunt*. His nostrils even flared a bit, like a cadaver dog.

His tone was highly accusatory. "You're the guy on Plugr."

My heart thudded. My brain cells instantly drained of all conscious matter. I was rude, screwed, and tattooed, run up against a slot canyon of spirituality, and the finger-pointing flash flood raging toward me was Crosley Shelvador.

CHAPTER THIRTEEN

Hunt

You're the guy on Plugr.

My mind whirled trying to put a fraction of logic together.

How would *this* dorky lunatic know I'd been in Plugr? Was he gay himself? That had to be it. But when I moved to ask him, Van butted in with,

"Crosley, my man. Let bygones be bygones. Besides, how do you remember what you saw weeks ago?"

With his next words, Crosley blew the cover completely. "Because who else is called StarGazer and looks like *this*?" He turned back to me. "You're a scientist, right?"

"Right," I said cautiously. "And yeah, I've been on Plugr before. Not at the moment." Was this weirdo just surfing around on Plugr? That was the only explanation. As I recalled, there *were* some pretty big lost causes there, and he would've been one of them.

Van put his hand on Crosley's arm. "All right. Let's not 'out' anyone, Crosley. Pinky, why don't we discuss Hunt's offer? What with the bathroom tiles and all —"

Pinky was eager too, trying to herd us out the back door toward the paperwork. "Yeah, Crosley, why don't you go get a pizza or something, do something useful while these men put together their offer —"

Crosley was relentless. Later on, I struggled trying to figure out if I was glad he pushed on, or not. Would I have been better off not knowing that Van the Man had catfished me over the coals unyieldingly, taking a sort of amusement out of the farce he'd been witness to? I could only be pleased there were just the four of us there, three of them laughing at my shame.

Crosley goofed, "So it worked out! I wondered if those Plugr things ever worked out. Course, I couldn't go for a guy. I'd try a girl, I guess."

Pinky shook Crosley's arm. "Yeah, that's an idea, Crosley. Try a dating app. I'm sure there's the exact girl there for a kook like you. Now we're in a rush—"

It was I who interrupted this time. "No. I want to know what this guy knows. Van, you saw me on the app? Who were you, then? What was your screen name?"

"He was Claude Berger!" Crosley busted out. "Aka SoulWrestler, didn't he tell you that on your first date?"

I held my palm to the ground. "Wait. *You* are SoulWrestler? We disconnected when you wanted a shirtless pic. How'd you find me down here?"

Crosley thought it was hilarious. "He was stalking you, man!"

"Shut up," I snapped at Crosley. Locking my eyes with Van's, I demanded again, "How'd you find me in Rough and Ready? Just some coincidence?"

Van stuttered. "Well, yeah, actually—we were invited to a fish fry down here, right Pinky?"

Pinky's eyes were like bowling balls. "Yeah. With the Zealots."

Van continued, "And we got to know them. And then, and then you walked in. So yeah, it was sheer coincidence. And I loved you, and I knew I'd blown it with that shirtless request, so I figured I'd get to know you all over again on my own terms."

I let that "I loved you" part roll right over me. I fisted my hands. "You catfished me. You pretended to be Claude Berger driving a delivery truck."

"Well—isn't that what most people do? Hide behind a profile until they're ready to come out, to reveal themselves to someone? And I felt I revealed myself to you."

"You created a catfishing account. You used photos of some random guy—who *is* Claude Berger, anyway? Who were those photos of?"

I knew I'd really hit a nerve. Van cringed back from me as though I were the North Wind. Pinky and even Crosley had gone completely stone solid by now, almost as though they were afraid of me. Was *I* fearsome? I'd never been before. I'd always been the "good parent," as in "I'll ask Dad and he'll say yes." But this being played for a reintarnated thrillbilly just chapped my hide. And I was tossing fear into Van's eyes.

"Claude Berger," he whispered, "was my lover in Hank's Hot Springs." His voice gained confidence and power as he spoke. "He was the first and *only* man I ever loved, so I used his photos and name. He was *murdered by Tyrone and Jackie Daytona* outside that fucking gay club I told you about. Beaten to fucking death before my very eyes. That's how far their hypocrisy extends, Hunt."

I fell back, strength draining from my limbs, but I was still angry. My need to express sorrow for his bereavement was weighted with my anger at being played for a fool. I growled, *"But you catfished me.* Made me start to fall in love with a lie." I hoped Van would let that "love" reference pass, too.

Van wiped his face with his hand. "I was a confused mess, Hunt. Still am. I came out here to fucking *kill* Tyrone and Jackie, and what have I done so far? Completely fucked the pooch when it came to shooting them. They were lurking around the club just *looking* for some gay men to murder, nothing better to do, it was a hobby of theirs, can you fucking understand that?"

Even Crosley nodded soberly. "Yeah. I need to learn more about that hobby."

Pinky said, "Van, you don't need to remember it so vividly if you don't want to."

But I was smoked. That murder had been ancient history for however long. *I* was right *now*, in front of his face, and he'd never come clean with me. "You're a fucking scam artist, Van! Who knows if that's even your fucking name!"

"It is," he whimpered.

I flung an arm and walked in little circles, and Pinky started exiting, hauling at Crosley's arm. Crosley, however, would not be dragged. His eyes were alight like a little boy at a construction site. He seemed to take pleasure in having caused this blowup, but I couldn't blame him. In a way, I should've thanked him.

Crosley said, "I don't want to have to listen to your real estate crap. Van needs me here."

"*No he doesn't!*" both Van and I shouted.

"Come on," said Pinky, yanking the guy's arm. "God relates to the real estate industry. He invented it."

The last thing Crosley said to me before Pinky whipped him out the sliding glass door was, "Are you going to drop space junk on American drug regulators?"

At last we were alone. I felt like I held a funeral for my humiliation. I could barely look at Van, as some of my rage had abated the more I thought of his dead lover. "SoulWrestler's face meant a lot to me. And now I find out it was all bullshit lies."

Van said earnestly, "Why do people catfish? Lack of confidence, Hunt! How could I come clean on Plugr when I lived with such a crowd of gay bashers? Look! Look what they did! They waited for us to walk into the alley and overwhelmed us with baseball bats, brass knuckles, and one guy even had nun chucks. It's been far too painful for me to think about, much less tell anyone. Rage fermented in the pit of my stomach until I got heartburn. Sometimes I thought I'd have a heart attack, like you did. I just wanted revenge, and I even wussied out on *that!*" Now *he* walked in circles, flailing his arms. I have to tell you, even in my anger-fueled confusion, I admired his ass.

I pointed a finger at him. "Your whole persona was the invention of a dissatisfied ghettobilly who became someone else! How can a person have a relationship with someone who never existed?"

Van grabbed a handful of his shirtfront. "But I'm here *now*, Hunt. This *is* the real me. I haven't lied to you since I met you face to face."

"You knew me as StarGazer, and you never admitted that! All the shit we shared? You knew it inside your head and were mocking me for it."

Van looked mournful. "*Why* would I mock you, Hunt? I love you."

A brief highly awkward pause ensued. I panted through my nostrils, my jaws firmly clenched. There was no way I could continue with this farce, not after having lost so much face, so what was my automatic response?

"Get out of my house!"

Much, much later I regretted this demand. But at the time, I was bleeding hurt from the realization that I'd been had. I'd been catfished and the culprit had been about to move into my new house with me.

The expression of shock and grief in Van's face was palpable. Maybe that's what prodded me to add, "I told you that I told my best friend I was gay, and his reaction—he ghosted me! I told you that we should meet with no agenda."

I could barely hear his muttered response, he was so deflated of pride. "And I asked for a shirtless pic."

I repeated it more robustly. "And you asked me for a shirtless pic!"

Van dredged up some sliver of self-esteem from the ghetto I'd thrown him into. "And *you* ghosted *me!*" He took a breath and quoted, "Even the moonlight will not deign to shine on an unfeeling person."

I waved his existence away. Repeated something I'd heard on Plugr. "Many men look attractive from afar. Get out of my fucking sight!"

I'd literally turned my back on Van. Maybe that gave him the gumption to say, "I don't know why you didn't give me a shirtless pic. You're the hottest muscle bunny I've seen, far or close. And you'll never find anyone else like me, far or close."

I could just *feel* his presence leave the kitchen. I had to lean on the stovetop and do some deep breathing to wipe the bubbles from my field of vision. I must've been holding my breath a lot of that time. My chest was so tight I feared another attack, and out of habit I felt around for my nitroglycerin pills *Whoops. Wrong house.* My meds, along with the entirety of my worldly possessions, were over at Fremont's house.

My worldly possessions. I'd been trying to arrange with Lauren a plan to remove my desk, tech equipment, and important books from my study. But first I needed a new address, so without emotion I slid open the screen door and went onto the patio.

Crosley Shelvador—his name reminded me of an old refrigerator I'd once had—had the nerve to be sitting at the patio table having a good old time with my realtor. I waved a dismissive hand at him.

"Get lost. Go back to your precious Society's Baggers."

He protested, as though I actually wanted to converse with him. "They're not *mine*. They're smelly, obnoxious, violent toolbags. I'm only informing on them."

I sat down by Pinky. "Oh, that makes it even better then."

Pinky gestured at Crosley. "Yeah, go. Go find Van the Man." She told me, "We saw him storming out the side gate a few minutes ago. I take it, it did not end well between you."

"You got it. Now, what are we gonna offer on this fine spread?"

CHAPTER FOURTEEN

Van

I felt like I'd been shot out of a cannon.

I'd been blown from this warm intimacy, this utterly tender, floating, womb-like dream I'd been living with Hunt, directly into a subterranean hell. I mean, this place I was in was worse than Hank's Hot Springs. Miles of ash pits, broken lawn mowers, and rivers of septic tank runoff would enhance the bottomless pit I now wallowed in.

Sure, the room at Royal and Berkeley's house was nice. Much nicer than my tomb at Jefferson's. The plywood walls were painted a trendy fog and I slept in a trendy mid-century double bed with matching dresser and nightstand straight from the Brady house. A triangular window under the eaves let in natural light. I genuinely dug these homes with their vibes of hibachi cooking, Ding Dongs and Cap'n Crunch for breakfast. I'd been starting to picture Hunt and me living the wholesome life, maybe even going to Lions crabfests like some of these Zealots did, Toys for Tots runs, farmer's markets. I would weld and repair every biker's scoot.

But the first thing I did when I returned to this room in my shame and horror was rip down the Queen poster.

I never wanted to see Brian Fucking May again.

I never wanted that stunning, pointed nose in my face again. Those angelic, chocolate brown eyes would never have to gaze upon the pitiful likes of me anymore. That blossoming baby gay could just go tangle with some other muscle bunny Tar Heel—but only if he wanted another crumbling, degraded criminal *such as me*.

The lowest of the low, I proceeded to flounder in my decline. I reveled in my own downfall, carrying around a mayonnaise jar of 128 proof Ole Smoky moonshine. Jamming my skullcap down to cover my patchy, drunken self-haircut, I operated in a floating haze I hoped that I'd forget. I knew I wasn't making a great impression on the Zealots, but I didn't much care. Sharing my time between Berkeley's house and an auto repair place on Surprise Street, my entire reality consisted of waxy smells, oily fingers, and stinging eyes. I even had a mind to off myself, but I was too lily-livered for that.

Even that infernal Maine Coon, Mighty, stopped coming around. Apparently canned salmon wasn't even good enough for him, he was probably so desperate to get away from a greasy bum like me. Together, Hunt and I had lured him in. Now my fishing skills lacked finesse, and I labored under a black cloud.

The only thing propping me up was planning the Kingman run.

Lock, Turk, their Sergeant-at-Arms Anson Dineyazzie and secretary Hobie Cleminshaw agreed to meet with me and Crosley at a bar, the Blue Oyster, in downtown Havasu. I recoiled with grief when it struck me it was a gay bar. I hadn't been inside one of those establishments since the last night of Claude's life.

"I . . . I don't know about this," I told Crosley as we removed our lids. He'd ridden "one up" with me down to Havasu, and that wasn't even one of the strangest things I'd done lately.

Crosley grinned, as always. "What's wrong? You weren't a fan of the Blue Öyster Cult?"

"What? No, I meant the guy in the tank top and the hat with the vinyl brim who just went inside." I steeled myself. I took a deep breath that made my lungs hurt with the fury of the cannabis smoke I'd been vaping.

Crosley said, "Well, his hat was kind of gay, but . . . *oh*, I see." He finally got it. "Well, you know it doesn't bother me. Here. I'll lead the way."

I have to say, it tickled me a little how boldly Crosley just sauntered on in there. It really didn't bother him in the slightest that there might be a guy with a limp wrist hoisting a drink with a little umbrella in it. He even waved at the Zealots, who were seated on the back patio, as though they fondly welcomed him. In fact, the opposite was true, as Lock sneered when we grabbed wrought iron chairs to sit.

"Crosley the Nark? Your reputation precedes you."

"I'll take that as a compliment. An orange juice," Crosley told the waiter.

I said, "Whiskey, neat."

Hobie Cleminshaw said, "Another lemon meringue martini." Hobie was a roly-poly very flaming sort of guy, but so far, I liked him.

Turk was no-nonsense, resembling a handsome, efficient vampire. "I'm telling you, Mr. Shelvador, I'm talking to you with extreme prejudice." He nodded at me. "I'm looking at possibly vetting Mr. Rossi here since he had a totally valid reason to be slumming with Society's Bag."

Lock added, "I'm sorry for your loss, man."

I nodded in acknowledgement. It was a given that the whole fucking world now knew about Claude's murder and my failed revenge scheme. Either Crosley or Pinky had broadcast it with a fucking megaphone, I didn't know who, and I didn't much care. It lent me legitimacy, that I'd earned sort of a chicken version of a Filthy Few patch. Maybe a filthy chicken patch.

I said, "Thanks for seeing us here today. I know there are a hundred reasons to be skeptical of Crosley here, but I think we should put faith in what he has to say about the Kingman run."

"All right," said Lock cautiously, "but we're going to take it with a grain of salt. We don't deal with pigs, and we don't deal with people who deal with pigs."

"That's a given," I agreed. "I've always hated pigs too." It was true. They were out to get me in Hank's Hot Springs.

All the paper money fluttering around the road in front of my house didn't help. I gestured at Crosley to speak.

He said, "Would it mitigate your fears to know that I was convicted of killing my own mother-in-law? I stabbed her in the chest twenty-eight times."

It was true. I hadn't told the Zealots that part, unsure how much it would really bolster their confidence in him.

The four bikers shared lidded looks. It was Anson who said, "You *do* understand we're not just in the randomly killing people business." The lethally gorgeous Anson had a Filthy Few patch, undermining his statement. He'd been overseas in Iraq, but I doubted they counted those guys they took to the ground before they'd joined the club.

Hobie argued with Anson. "Well, it *is* impressive he's willing to go to those lengths."

Turk slapped the table. "Whatever. We're here to get intel on the Kingman run, and we can evaluate later the veracity of his statements."

I was always impressed these guys used words like "veracity." They weren't your garden variety biker club, for sure.

Crosley said, "Then hear this. I listened in while the Prez, Tyrone Shoelaces, and the Sergeant-at-Arms, Jackie Daytona, discussed jumping you in Kingman, surprise blasting you all at once to make some sort of idiotic statement."

Turk wiggled his eyebrows. "And the goal?"

"Goal is to jump you and take your backpacks, your cuts, whatever they can get their hands on. Take your scoots to humiliate you in public. Word of their deed will travel far and wide."

Lock snorted. "Well. Let's see how well *that* goes over. I've heard the Baggers are all meth heads who play pool all day. Anorexic little white worms."

I inserted, "Well. They're worms for sure, but they know how to rumble. As both Crosley and I have seen firsthand, they resort to low blows like nun chucks and brass knuckles."

The Bent Zealots shared a chuckle. Hobie Cleminshaw said, "We're not above grabbing a hubcap or tailpipe to whale on a foe."

"I'm saying they have this simmering inner rage, probably the result of dysfunctional childhoods." I took my whiskey from the waiter and gulped. I'd been drinking so much it failed to affect me anymore, as though I'd built up a tolerance to it.

The Zealots still laughed. "Don't we all?" Anson said, smiling genuinely for the first time.

How could I get it through to them that they might lose this round? And to a club of such whining, lazy, vengeful dirtbags. "Listen. You should take this seriously. I've seen them kill a man with nunchucks. I mean, just cave his skull in till his eyeballs were mashed potatoes." *That* made them sit up a bit. I had not wanted to dredge up vibrant memories of Claude, but I did what I had to do all in the name of survival.

Turk said, "I get it, man. You're right, we should take this more seriously. Shelvador, did you hear anything about where they might do this? Which day during the run?"

Crosley blathered, "Tuesday, the big day. They'll send someone out to trail you, get you when you're all in one area."

Anson said, "We'll be at that Route 66 diner that day. Planning the exact path of our daily run."

Turk nodded. "Forewarned is forearmed."

"It'd be good if we had a mole who could keep us updated," said Lock. "Shelvador, any chance you could get back in good with those guys? Maybe hand them some fake intel about us."

"That's a definite maybe," Crosley said. "Believe you me, I've been wracking my brains trying to find a way. My parole officer said they might remand me back into custody if I can't give them any more dirt on the Baggers."

I said, "Well, keep us out of it. The last thing we need is a bunch of pigs arresting us because we're defending ourselves against some gay bashers."

Turk nodded at me. "Defending ourselves. I like that."

"Yeah," said Anson. "Defending ourselves. That's what we're doing, all right."

"I want to be there," I blurted. All heads turned to me. I gulped more whiskey so I wouldn't stutter. "You can figure out why. I'm out bad because I tried and failed to shoot that fucker Jackie Daytona in the back of the head while he was sucking dick like a hypocrite."

Turk said, "Yeah. Everyone deserves a second chance."

The men nodded, and there was a brief silence, like a prayer for the soul of Claude Berger.

I added, "I've got a bunch of iron in a truck in the Methodist parking lot. You can have it all."

Turk raised an eyebrow. "From . . . .?"

"Yes," I clipped.

Turk and the other three shared looks. It seemed they had a new appreciation for me.

CHAPTER FIFTEEN

Hunt

I moved through life like an automaton—without emotion, hopes, or desires. Because to desire something or hope beyond hope meant a giant bringdown was in store for you. The simple solution was to never yearn.

The seller accepted my offer on the house, after forcing me to overbid the asking price by $30,000 due to some other motherfuckers bidding it up. Okay, they were just a family wanting a safe home in a secure district full of criminal bikers. I was just angry with the world so everyone was pretty much a motherfucker to me.

My work at the missile range had already started with a glorious rocket launch. The hot pink glow as the vapor payload surged into the near-vacuum of space, visible from Havasu and Phoenix. I had a lot going on, and too much time to think when I rode my Dyna Wide Glide back to my new home, so I started accepting fourteen-hour shifts.

The betrayal by Van—by SoulWrestler—cut me deeper than my divorce. I'd imagined I loved a man who turned out to be a shirtless pic-asking slut, which made me a slut too, just like my reprehensible father. My isolation and skin hunger hadn't abated though, so like a true slut I jacked off a lot, looking at photos of studs, although definitely not on Plugr.

My crashing downfall was that Van had been living a lie, portraying himself as a different person. He even planned on moving in with me without telling me he was SoulWrestler. *When would that come into the open?* That he'd been privy to my cringe-inducing DMs regarding my sappy divorce, my sappy children, my sappy job. We'd both originated from North Carolina, but had branched off on utterly separate paths. I'd lifted myself out of the scum, while Van had wallowed in it. I'd gone on to soar at Princeton, and Van had dodged SWAT, hiding in the sewers of Hank's Hot Springs.

Yet our divergent roads had united again in Rough and Ready . . .

I was glad I hadn't told Lauren about Van. She had moved with Hannah back to Pensacola, Florida where they'd made many friends in the military when I worked there. The regimented, preprogrammed life benefited them, where the entire city was like one big happy tribe served to you on a plate. I realized my future Bent Zealot existence would be like that, too. I dared to yearn for a new built-in family with those men, so I hung out at The Happy Hour, just breathing in and exuding the biker life. I even got a black leather vest, though mine had no patch, not even a PROSPECT one.

And Mighty returned to me. Maybe that had something to do with Van being gone. Mighty started coming several times a day—I fed him only a tablespoon of wet food at a time for fear of messing with his wild diet—and eventually he let me pet him. I nearly broke down and cried. He pressed his butt against my hand, and was that a purr I heard? I collapsed slowly into my midcentury patio chair, and Mighty looked up at me with wonder, as though seeing me for the first time.

Maybe he *did* see me for the first time. I'd left behind any pretense at family life, yet I'd continued working on rockets, ever tightening my scientific skills. I still looked at planets and satellites through my telescope, now in the still Carolina Blue bowl of the sky above our suburb. I was the same, yet different, no longer the Plugr-surfing local yokel, but a sophisticated, stargazing, reluctantly abstinent biker.

Always on the alert at seeing Van in The Happy Hour. Pinky calmed my fears on that.

"He's completely hit the skids," she told me as she wiped down the bar. Yes, she tended bar sometimes for the club, but because she *wanted* to. They probably paid her in wine—rosé, because that was the drink of the worldly realtor. "I can't even talk to him anymore. He utters monosyllables like a bumper sticker. He's a zombie, Hunt." She paused her wiping and looked at me, lips pursed. "And I think there's something you can do about it."

"Not me. He scammed me, Pinky. I feel like the biggest ditchpig on the planet."

"Huntington," she said, using my full legal name, "it's just your ego that's been bashed."

"'Just?" I cried. "Isn't that bad enough? It's like my mother all over again, browbeating me into submission." I realized I'd used BDSM terms, so I couldn't look Pinky in the eye.

She wagged the rag at me. "See? You're overly sensitive in that area. Van is *not* your mother. Van is Van. I'm telling you, Huntington. In all my dealings with Society's Bag, he is the most tenderhearted, profound fellow in all of Arizona. You need to give him more credit. So he catfished you, big deal. Don't lots of people online hide behind fake personas? And look at his reasoning. He lived with *the people who murdered his boyfriend*. Think about that."

I waved a dismissive hand. "I do." It was true. My own egotism hung over my head like a noose. It took precedence over Van's anguish, his thorough torment at having witnessed his lover murdered in front of his eyes. A larger and larger chunk of my guilt told me to cut him some slack. We'd been planning to meet face to face, anyway. I would've noticed he didn't resemble the Claude Berger photos he'd posted. No. He was better. Bigger guns, shapelier mouth, most angelic head of curls . . .

Pinky was talking. "I'm telling you, Hunt, his bravery knows no bounds. So he choked when making a hit on Jackie Daytona, big deal. It just shows his humanity! This isn't civilized people we're dealing with here, Hunt. It's the biker world."

I thumped my empty whiskey glass on the bar and exhaled my last sip at Pinky to indicate I wanted another. "I've become too soft, Pinky. I'm like a gentleman gangster. I need to stand up for myself, be more barbaric. I need to blend in, the kind of banging hot aggressive archangel Van always said I was. Unless he was lying," I added.

Pinky frowned as she went to get the whiskey bottle. I knew she was about to spout something fresh at me, so I was relieved when the front door swung open, admitting Fremont and Noel. Fremont lit up when he saw me and came over.

"Well, my stargazing friend."

Ouch. It hurt that he'd—on purpose or not—called me my Plugr name. So I said, "Well, my radium-cleaning-up friend. What's on your agenda tonight? I'm off work until Wednesday."

"You're not coming on the Kingman run tomorrow?"

I had a bad feeling someone would ask me that. "Ah . . . you know how it goes. Not looking forward to running into a certain catfisher."

Pinky helped me out on that one. "Van would never go, Hunt. Between swilling bum wine and fixing everyone's rides, he's busy as a one-legged cat in a sandbox. Go. Go with Fremont and Noel. Give some air to your new leather cut."

"Yeah!" said Fremont, slapping me on the shoulder. "Blow some dust from your soul. You gotta be back at work Wednesday? You can do it. And who knows? You'll see your intended, Van the Man."

I made a lip fart with whiskey. "Not likely, Fremont. Not after what he did to me."

"*What*? He created a fake persona for a dating app. Big fucking deal. I'll bet that goes on more often than not. Are you in love with him?"

Of course I was going to change the subject, but Pinky filled in for me. "He's madly in love, this knucklehead. Why do you think Van's been getting basted on hootch and this guy's got his head stuck in a telescope? Because they both love each other. It's the way of the world."

"Look, look." Fremont murmured, taking the barstool next to me.

Oh, no. A lecture.

"Tending your wounds will hurt for a while. But often I can find this key to climb down, down into my depths where I see an image of my future sleeping in the dark mirror. All I have to do is bend over that dark mirror and see my own image. But now I completely resemble the Future Me. My brother, my master."

I rolled my eyes, and Pinky said, "Wow. That's heavy, Mr. Uranium Man. You've been hanging out with that pastor husband of yours too much."

"What do you say?" Fremont asked.

"Uranium on the brain," I said. "Look. I'll ride to Kingman with you guys. But I'm not going to go out of my way to accommodate that scumbag."

Fremont said, "Watch what you call your future husband."

Pinky said, "Future *ex*-husband is more like it, the venom this guy spews."

So I went on the run with them.

Kingman gave us a chance to reconnect with our brother clubs, the Bare Bones, the Pure and Easy "Red Rocks Originals" as well as the Tucson and Flagstaff chapters. It was a superb ride up the Purple Heart Trail in formation with my brothers. Fremont and Noel rode point, Antonio and Kingsley rode sweep, placing me in their midst, as though protecting me.

And I suppose they were.

They took a chance on an inexperienced rider like me, and it felt fantastic. I didn't carry a piece, even after doing gun range runs with Fremont during off-work hours. I hadn't practiced lately so I turned down the offer to carry a Glock. I just rumbled through that desert, my forearms dangling from my ape hangers, eyes protected by Oakley shades.

That hour-long ride imbued me with the proper amount of bravery, the swagger to mingle with the hardest asses in Kingman. Sure, my velvet pants weren't the norm, and the talismans, minerals, and bones I wore around my neck displayed in the deep V of my T-shirt were not the typical biker wear. But everyone seemed to know and respect that the Bent Zealots were different.

We rolled down the main drag, rumbling out our presence, sneering our dominance at every pedestrian. When we stopped for a beer, the bar was so packed we had to take our cups onto the sidewalk—probably legal only during our annual presence—and my brothers in arms yammered a giant load of knowledge into my head. The run was a coming together of music, motorcycles, and metal.

"Those twatwaffles with Disney swords on their backpatch?" Antonio pointed with his beer cup. "Those are Cutlasses, mortal enemies of the Bare Bones, so therefore mortal enemies of ours. And anyone with a Dotards cut is a rival."

Kingsley added, "But not during the Kingman run. It's unseemly to trash the goodwill of the Kingman Board of Supervisors by popping anyone off. We stay civilized and courteous during this run."

Antonio's beer cup shoved aside Kingsley's. "Except not with that cockbite Dagwood." The cockbite swaggering past a toy shop boasted patches that declared him a Hellfire Nut. Antonio informed me, "They motored our man Ormond in a sneak attack, so that assclown is fair game."

"Oh yeah?" I'd become fairly proficient in the Brazilian *jiu jitsu* during my late teens, discovering a mixed martial arts "sport" that resonated with me. I could take down Dagwood with a chokehold. Then I realized that would just start an all-out war, and we weren't here for that—although I'd heard a few words of discontent saying otherwise. "Has anyone seen a Society's Bagger yet?"

We'd all been briefed on the possibility that the Baggers would jump us today. I wasn't present in the chapel when Turk and Lock handed everyone this intel. But Fremont gave me the lowdown later. It had something to do with a diner on Highway 66 being a very public spot for the Baggers to stake their claim, show off their power. Fremont had asked me at the time if I wanted a piece for protection and I'd said no.

Now in front of the bar, I sought him out.

"Hey. About that gun . . ."

"Sure." Fremont was on top of things, as always. Open carry was legal in Arizona, so we went to his scoot in an alley, where he unlocked his saddlebags. "I'm glad you're reconsidering."

"Well, it's been a long time since we went to the range . . ."

"Yeah. And you were really proficient then."

I couldn't resist swelling with pride. Seemed I had so little to swell about lately. "I *do* spend a lot of time looking through scopes, being exacting about my aim." I referred to telescopes, but Fremont had to chuckle.

"Here's a .380 pistol, a Ruger."

"No Glock?" I frowned. I liked the idea, the image of carrying a Glock. Already becoming indoctrinated into the club's way of thinking.

Fremont said, "Not on me, although Van gave the club a huge stash of — oh, never mind."

I frowned as I slid the barrel of the Ruger into my waistband, biker style. "Huge stash of what?"

"Apparently he was the armament manager for the Baggers. When he bailed on them, he took a truck full of iron. Gave it to us a couple days ago."

"Hmph. What a guy."

Fremont frowned. "Hunt. You have to get over the catfishing thing. Van appears to be the real thing, a genuine ace. There's talk of giving him a Prospect patch once he shows his mettle."

I put my hands on my hips. "A Prospect patch? Hey, I didn't work undercover with a rival club. I'm a real doctor, just like Thymus Moog." Dr. Moog was an MD, a cardiologist, an original founding member—and a complete whackjob. I grasped for straws, I knew.

"Well, you better remember. Never let a patchholder hit the ground. Van is supposed to show up at the diner because he wants a chance to confront those murderers. We're eager to give him his chance."

I looked at the ground. "Yeah. He really needs to even the score." But wouldn't that lead to bloodshed, something we wanted to avoid? If I didn't foresee bloodshed, why did I ask Fremont for protection?

The milling scene in the diner around me changed from one of jovial camaraderie to looming, ominous doom, and I couldn't eat. Even the coffee made me nauseous. I nudged Noel off the bench and shoved my way down the crowded aisle. Someone had said the Bagger's call to action had pinged the pig's radar. Someone said normally they were very friendly, not wishing to get on our bad side. And two Zealots—looked like Dr. Moog and Mayo Snodgrass—were stationed in a Honda Accord.

Out front, some guys were toking weed in the open, and for the hundredth time, I wished that stuff agreed with me. It just made me paranoid. I talked to Ormond, Anson Dineyazzie's husband. Word had it he was a badge slut, and had serviced some of these pigs before hooking up with Anson.

"I heard you're not a big fan of the Hellfire Nuts," I said as a conversation opener.

A lush, gorgeous Milanese runway model, skin tawny and glowing, Ormond simmered naked under his cut. He stood with thumb hooked into his back jeans pocket, eyes scanning an unseen horizon. He didn't glance at me before saying, "Yeah. Four of them jumped me in my studio." Ormond did special effects makeup for films. "Reamed the shit out of me while calling me a fag."

Reamed? Did he mean what I thought he meant? I was saved from making an awkward response when Ormond jerked his cellphone up, read the screen, then showed it to me.

Baggers are rolling southwest down 66 from flea market, Dr. Moog and Rover were informing us.

Our eyes looked to the northeast, seeing only single-story buildings, chain-link fences, tractors for rent. Telephone poles told us that this place wasn't fully modern. Signs for Mountain Dew and bale grass for your horse.

Ormond said, "If you're not packing, you should go inside."

"I'm packing," I said, in what I hoped was a cocksure voice. Would I really use my piece? What gripe did I have against the Baggers? I realized that I had plenty of gripe, reasons to take them out. They had murdered Van's boyfriend violently in front of his very eyes. If Van wasn't there to exact his revenge — and I hadn't seen him yet — I could do it for him.

What I saw next threw me completely off whatever little game I had.

The Baggers rolled, pipes rumbling. It struck me how similar we all were, killing each other just due to our different patches. Only a few Baggers wore lids, some with flowing hair like mine. Some were porky like Hobie Cleminshaw, their guts protruding from under their too-small T-shirts. A couple muscle daddies and gym bunnies — straight, of course — glared at us. The club was composed of all kinds, overall cruder, less schooled, brimming with white man's grievance.

I assumed Tyrone Shoelaces rode point in their thundering formation. Wearing no helmet, he had a chubby, impudent face, like his shit didn't stink. It seemed that his eyes were glued on me, of all people. I knew they somehow thought I could help their Sergeant-at-Arms with drugs for his back, very logical since I was a doctor. Maybe he looked greedily at the pockets of opiates I had.

As Ormond thumbed his phone, more Zealots poured from the diner. Lock even had a paper napkin stuck in his waistband, and Hobie hadn't finished the biscuit in his hand. It would come down to which side had more people, so I counted them. Twenty-three Harleys.

We had more than twenty-three—we had rough Bare Bones elders Tuzigoot and Duji, as well as younger studs like Roman and Knoxie. I thought of the piece in my waistband, felt the heft, the metal, mentally eyeballed it. But it wasn't time yet for gun play, as the Baggers now rumbled to a stop on the road's shoulder. This allowed one more scoot to come from behind, a real shocker.

Crosley fucking Shelvador. That fucking narc. A hush came over our parking lot.

"See?" Crosley yelled. "I showed you where they are."

Yet, in another frightening move, Crosley continued racing his scoot toward us!

"Thanks for waiting for me, Turk, Lock!" Crosley crowed. To add another layer of shock to the unfolding scene, Crosley fishtailed his rear so he faced the Baggers, dismounted his ride, and Turk and Lock slapped him on the back! They practically gave him a thug hug!

"*You fucking traitor!*" bellowed Tyrone.

And it was *on.*

A Bagger gave an uppercut to a Zealot's jaw. *Twinkletoes! They had to pick on Twinkletoes!* Couldn't they see he was disabled? But that wouldn't make a difference to these twisted fuckwads.

Jiu jitsu had taught me the most inefficient way to fight someone was to stand off trading punches. Protecting my face with my upper arms, I moved into a clinch with a smelly guy. I lifted and folded him, taking the fight to the ground. Once I was dominant, I mounted him and hooked my ankles under his knees, nailing him with my entire weight. This prevented him from punching me or throwing me off, so psychologically he was already ruined.

It worked. He weakened as the will ebbed from his limbs, so I pulled back and smashed my fist into his nose. The cartilage crunched under my knuckles, but thinking of Van, I pummeled him again—maybe three or four times, I don't know, I was so enraged, like cocaine jolted through my nervous system.

I sprang to my feet, dragging Twinkletoes to stand. Only when I looked at his spindly biceps did I realize my hand was bloody. "Are you sure you wanna do this?"

He shook himself free of me. "I can protect myself!" he pouted.

Meanwhile, Zealots rushed from the diner's hovel like coyotes on rabbits. One Zealot brained a Bagger with a coffee cup. A few Baggers had brought chains, whipping them like we were cattle. That clanking cowed us for a few seconds, then Tuzigoot caught ahold of a chain in his fists, yanked the holder flat on his back, and jumped on his ribs till they crunched.

A Bagger smashed an outdoor chair over Kingsley's head. I turned to the left to see a Bagger equipped with brass knuckles crunch Berkeley's cheekbone into smithereens. Yet Twinkletoes was right—he could kick ass with the best of them, and soon was stomping up and down on a facedown Bagger. And the gangly, uncoordinated Crosley hammered away at a brother's face as the guy splayed on a car's hood. So much blood spurted from the guy's head it looked like Jackson Pollock had wandered by to splatter a masterpiece.

I had only beaten one guy, so I looked around for someone not waging war. Turned out to be Tyrone Shoelaces, eyes bulging from his head at the sight of me, hands stiff as claws. "*You!*"

I put my hand to my chest and frowned. Me? Why? A gunshot somewhere to my right made my ears ring. All bets were off.

"You're the doctor we were supposed to get medicine from! You're in cahoots with the Chinese!"

What in the name of all things sacred?

I was a tall target, so I reached for my Ruger while ducking. I would bash the wind out of Tyrone with a crushing full mount, shoot if I had to, but that pasty bastard was faster than me! The last thing I remember is looking down his barrel while he loomed over me—I hadn't evaded his technique of drawing and shooting.

To my credit, I did squeeze my trigger. But by then, someone hit me from the side so speedily, with such force, my boots left the ground.

I uttered "*oomph*" before I slammed into the blacktop. My attacker zipped faster than a toupee in a hurricane, because a split second later this guy leveled *his* piece at Shoelaces and blew a hole right through the Bagger's forehead. I imagined I could hear the "splat" when brains and bones exploded from the back of his skull. All action surrounding us came to a dead stop as though someone had hit the pause button. Tyrone did that thing where a corpse stands still for a few split seconds, even gets a little cross-eyed. Van and I held our breaths.

Maybe I dreamed it, but there seemed to be a realization in Tyrone's eyes that he'd seen his maker before he thudded to the asphalt like a dissolving snowman.

Someone hit the play button. Men resumed bashing each other with embarrassing items. Hobie's biscuit went flying. Yet the gunplay was murderous. Another leather cut-wearing biker was flung facedown over Tyrone as though salaaming to the fuckwad's memory.

"Come on," said Van, kneeling and shaking me. "You're a giant fucking bullseye for these assclowns."

"I *have* a piece," I protested. "And what about Jackie Daytona?" I knew he wanted revenge on Daytona as well. I was becoming very world-weary already in this biker club.

"No!" barked Van. "I'm getting you the fuck out of here!"

Van folded me in his arms as we ducked and ran. Bullets cracked everywhere, shattering the diner window, thudding into cars unlucky enough to be in the parking lot. Another

Bagger looked dead, flat on his back with his tongue oozing from his mouth. Anson helped a bloody Bond scurry behind the diner wall. Van did the Clint Eastwood thing of peeking out from behind the corner and squeezing off a few shots before flinching and racing back to me. He didn't seem to care about Bond's predicament.

He only had eyes for me.

"Hunt, Hunt, Hunt," he said over and over, smearing my hair back from my face. "How'd you get involved in something this stupid? You're not stupid. Why would you put yourself in so much danger?"

My answer was swift. "I wanted to get revenge for you." I inhaled and exhaled. "Because I love you."

Soon the commotion of the rumble was behind us. This time Van rode back home two up behind me.

CHAPTER SIXTEEN

Van

Something fundamental happened between us on the ride back to Rough and Ready. The straight road had me hypnotized as we sped into a naked sunset, my arms clamped around my beloved's narrow waist. Everything seemed so obvious, so right. I laughed inside wondering how I had ever doubted anything.

I desired Hunt. I longed for him. I wasn't afraid to put my heart into his hands because I trusted him. I knew he wouldn't stomp on me. Nothing bad would come of our love. *Our love.* Hunt had told me he loved me.

I didn't question it—I didn't doubt it.

No, it was all too real to me, and that oddly made it more comforting . . . more tender and warming. To feel loved was to feel pride, confidence, and serenity. I recalled my recovering friends in the holler mentioning those things, stuff they had to find within themselves to get their lives back on track. I was already one step ahead because *Hunt loved me.* I loved him right back. I proved it by getting him the hell out of that bullet-crazed parking lot.

Shit, I had blasted Tyrone Shoelaces right through the old noggin. What a powerful feeling, his very existence in my hand. The look in his eyes right before I squeezed the trigger was priceless. Tyrone had caved in Claude's exquisite face with nun chucks while a couple of mindless goons—Needle Dick Nick and Gangbang Greg, I believe—held me tight, helpless. So the divine chance to plug Tyrone right through the skull meant holy payback. Does it sound thuggish that the squish of his bones and brains spraying felt so just, so right?

After secreting Hunt around the corner, I'd picked off a couple other Baggers. Needle Dick Nick whacked Rover with a baseball bat when I got him right in the throat. No ever-lovin' way in God's good heaven he survived his carotid artery bursting all over another Bagger's white shirt. I didn't have time to chuckle before nailing George Zip plumb through the heart. Again, I was damn sure he couldn't exist long with a quarter-sized hole in his aorta as the whole structure flopped around in protest. I'd seen it with my own eyes in Hank's Hot Springs. The guy's heart flapped for maybe fifteen more seconds—on the *outside* of his chest—and both him and George Zip were flat on their backs in no time.

I don't know who shot at me then, but I ducked down around the corner, letting the bullet explode bricks. I covered my beloved Hunt with my body, instructing him to *never* put his archangel self into the line of fire again. Yes, that's when he told me he loved me, and it didn't take many IQ points to jump into his nearby Harley saddle and fishtail it out of there. The Zealots would know I didn't abandon them after taking three Baggers to the ground. I'd done my share, especially for a guy who'd been Myrtle Beach drunk on shine for several weeks now.

I hadn't imbibed that morning, knowing I would pop up in Kingman to make my stand. There was no way I had foreknowledge Hunt would be there. I hadn't planned the whole thing that way, to sweep in like some kind of warped savior to scurry his ass out of the line of fire. But it worked.

As I'd hoped, we pulled into the driveway of Hunt's new house. Dismounting, I ran my fingers through what was left of my hair. I looked to Hunt. His long legs swung off the saddle, and he shook his waves out of the lid. I hadn't worn a lid and who cared with my patchy self-haircut.

He stood there with flowing locks, tantalizing tufts peeking above the V in his T-shirt. The tokens, badges and relics he boasted around his neck were symbols of his deep, thoughtful intellect. He loved me, but it hurt to face him.

He smiled. "Let's go inside. I need a drink."

I sighed with gratitude. "Yeah. I sure don't. Won't, for another few months at least."

Hunt chuckled, rustling his keys as we headed for his front door. "I heard you were downing all kinds of Night Train bottles."

"More like Thunderbird."

"You know it's bad when you open a bottle of MD 20/20 Blue Raspberry."

"Sounds like your Princeton days."

"No. We were more highfalutin. Mountain Dew and gin."

I entered the hallway, transfixed at the change in the place. Hunt had created a minimalist mid-century place for himself.

A braided wicker lamp hung from the entry hall ceiling. A geometric runner led to the right, past the family room where a rounded rosewood table flaunted several chairs that looked to be carved of a single piece of wood. I wasn't familiar with the artwork on the walls. That was one of my failings from my holler days. I had money, but who cared about artwork? Heading to the kitchen, through the sliding glass door, I spied an enormous telescope on a tripod. I wanted to know more about his interests. I really did.

Hunt slid one of the plywood cabinet doors aside and withdrew a bottle of bourbon. I watched him pour and sip without a single craving hitting me. I just admired his cupid lips, his Adam's apple bobbing as he gulped. He wore a cut without a single patch. I admired the sluggish outline of his cock nestled up against his hip. *I have sucked that big old horse cock.*

"I'm glad you got this house. You deserve to join the Bent Zealots."

"My wife sent over whatever furnishings she could. I don't know what use to the Zealots I could be."

I had to guffaw. "You could spy on the Chinese. Bomb the FDA. Make fentanyl."

Hunt was a damned god when he smiled. "Is that what Jackie Daytona said I could do?"

"Yep."

"If you catfished me."

Oh, here we fucking go again. I'd never live that down. But I had to address it. "Yeah. Crosley Shelvador caught me drooling over you, so they took the ball and ran with it."

"So it was their idea to catfish me."

"Yes. No. It's something I would've done anyway, Hunt. You were the most fucking gorgeous hunk of stud I'd seen in all of Plugr, and if I couldn't have you, why I'd—"

"Dive into a vat of shine?"

I smiled, relieved he took it so lightly. "I'd follow you to Kingman and save you from an enemy's bullet."

"Which you did. I don't know what I was doing there, playing with the big boys. Trying to prove myself." He gulped the last of his booze and poured himself another. He offered the bottle to me, and I shook my head.

I said, "You want to join the club. That's natural, to want to prove yourself. I see you got yourself a piece."

Hunt nodded, taking the iron from his waistband and laying it on the counter. "I only got off one shot, have no idea what I hit, if anything." He looked levelly at me, eyeballs dilating. "Not like you. How many did you put under?"

I puffed up at that. "Three, including that worthless cocksucker Tyrone Shoelaces." I set my piece on the counter next to his, like two gunfighters going inside a western saloon.

"I wonder who got Jackie Daytona."

We spoke in a mind-blowing way. A month ago we were pointless, wandering seekers, fishing for feral cats, for each other. We needed to shake off our gigantic, burdensome pasts. Now we discussed offing rivals with comfort.

Gaining confidence, I said, "I'll give *you* a shirtless pic." In one fluid motion I whipped off my grimy T-shirt and ran my fingers through my curly chest hair. "It's only fair. Here. Take a picture. You can even see my real face. No more Claude Berger."

Damnation, did my sensuous archangel waste no time snatching his phone and taking pix of me. "Awesome," he said, clicking away. "SoulWrestler, you might've been down, but you're not out. You're so buff, you make a man want to cry. I can't fucking resist—"

And his words were swallowed when he dove in face first to my chest.

Clamping his mouth around my nipple, he swished his tongue-tip around the hard nubbin. Oh my saints, did that sensation go straight to my cock. I had to grip his biceps to hold him at bay, that's how packed my balls filled.

But as I pressed his torso from me, he glued his hips to mine. *Oh. My. Saints.* I'd been dreaming of this during drunken jackoff sessions, and now it really happened. I felt the entire breadth and length of his horse cock plastered to mine. We both dressed to the right so Hunt angled his hips just to thrust his hardon to me. This banging hot astrophysicist chewed on my nipple and dry humped me for all he was worth. Like the floodgates opened and we no longer had to pretend we didn't give a fuck about the other.

The stiff rim of his glans rubbed against mine, coaxing precome, where I knew it made a darker spot against my jeans. I didn't care. I gasped and groaned now, uttering stupid words I didn't mean, like, "Oh, God, no. No, Hunt. Jesus, stop. You're driving me apeshit. Fuck, I'm gonna come in my pants. Stop, ya'll. You fucking ghettobilly. Driving me over the edge."

To my shock, Hunt did stop. His mysterious grin told me he was up to something good as he slunk from the kitchen. An idiotic smile adorned my face as I stared mindlessly at the bourbon bottle. I didn't need no hootch to submit to what Hunt had in mind.

Submit to. Wait, wasn't *I* the Dom in this pairing?

Hunt returned in a flash. I admired his bulging bicep vein as he fiddled with something small, taking the opportunity to slide my palm up his concave four-pack and tweak his nipple.

He grimaced with pleasure. "Ah." But he didn't stay distracted for long, as he clamped something piercing and metallic on my nipple.

My turn to gasp. "Land's sake!" He'd gone and grabbed one of those small alligator clips used for electronics testing. I used a lot of them in my auto shop. Never had it occurred to me to use them as nipple clamps, and I burst out with, "You fuckin' beelzebubba! What the hell you stickin' on my chest? I'm supposed to be the one punishing *you*, you fuckin' clem!"

The sly grin never left his face as he slid both palms down my backside, embracing me to him. The alligator clips lost importance when he touched his nose to mine, lapping at my upper lip like a cat. "I love you, you fuckin' clem." His hands swept lower, squeezing my ass cheeks. Separating them, he slipped a few fingers into my crack while rubbing his chest to mine. It felt like he had pierced my very nipples, lightning bolts shooting through them and straight to my prick, which pulsed with need.

Clawing his T-shirt out of the way, I too slid one hand under his belt, his powder-soft pants. His ass cheek was gorgeous and muscular, honed in steroids and maintained with power. My other hand undid his turquoise and silver belt buckle, scrabbling for the steamy root of his cock.

Hunt gasped into my mouth. I took a few bites out of his upper lip too and replied, "I'm madly in love with you." I silenced any non-response with a kiss that overwhelmed even his fingers toying with his clamps. *I* needed to be in control, not him. Yet I didn't want to remove the clamps, they were maintaining my lust so close to the tipping point.

When I squeezed his hot, bulbous corona in my palm, he'd had enough. With one last bite to my lower lip, he dropped to his knees.

Unprepared to be worshipped like this, I fell back against the counter. I'm sure my guttural groan could be heard down the fucking street as I grasped for the edge, holding myself up, just barely. Hunt inhaled the length of my dick, even gulping the jet of precome that spurted. I tried to relax into it, the loose electrical leads dangling down to my pubic bone.

But it was fuckin' difficult. I struggled. Hunt's warm, suckling mouth worshipped at my very shrine, in control of all sensation. I was king of the world, desired by such a king as him. He twirled his tongue up and down my shaft, into my slit, using the slickness to arrow a finger down my perineum, teasing me to the maximum. I couldn't tear my eyes from his beauty, riveted to the point of his nose, the silk of his lashes, the depth and fullness of his hair when I speared my fingers through it.

My knees began to collapse as he teased me over the cliff. I knew I didn't want this—didn't want to shoot my load into his loving mouth! I wanted to fuck the daylights out of him, to nail him to the floor while spanking that luscious, muscular ass. I even tried thinking of repulsive things to avoid my imminent release, but these items flitted out of my brain as fast as I forced them in. It was all over. The nipple clamps did their job.

Load after load spewed into my lover's mouth. He took it like a champ, gulping and snorting, massaging the root of my dick, pumping me for more. As for me, I just fucking held my breath waiting for it to subside, that's how intense it felt. My cock twitched and pulsed and it seemed to never recede. Hunt's hand pulled the loose lead to my left nipple. I jumped with such intensity I arched my hips, shoving my boner into Hunt's hot mouth.

He tweaked the right tit. I fixed to begin another orgasm anew. A great payload of jizz erupted, sending a tidal wave of ecstasy surging through my groin.

Hunt stayed with it, torturing my nipple with just the right panache. Damnation, that man was made for men, a natural born star at this. *And I'm putty in his hands.*

At last he detached his mouth with a giant slurp. He speared his fingers through his mane of hair to brush it from his face. When he looked up at me, his devilish grin floored me. I finally let my breath go in a giant whoosh, and became so lightheaded I had to stumble to the kitchen table and sit, yanking up my pants on the way and stuffing my throbbing dick where it had been.

I flung myself back like a wiped-out prizefighter, one hand on my abdomen, the other fingertips brushing the floor tiles. That hoodbilly Hunt, he just had to stalk on over and swing one boot so he straddled me. Enormous stiff pecker in my face, he maintained his dominance by splaying his fingers on each temple of mine and thrusting that erection against my mouth.

My mouth actually watered. I grabbed his hips like a football and opened wide to inhale a mouthful of that delicious meat.

But Hunt stepped back.

What a fucking backwoods clem. He leaned against a wall of cabinets, knowing full damn well his jutting hips displayed the outline of that swollen penis, commanding my entire attention. My entire being.

His crossed arms served as a frame for this savory vision. "Which nipple is more sensitive?" he demanded.

"What? Uh, I guess the right."

That seemed to please Hunt. "Okay then. We'll have Knoxie pierce that one. Put a barbell through it."

"Who's Knoxie?" I didn't argue with the piercing.

"The Bare Bones over in Pure and Easy. He's their tattoo artist."

I grinned, still panting. "You're becoming quite the biker. Want to bet they'll let you prospect before me?"

"I wouldn't be too sure. You earned your Filthy Few patch today."

Hunt was right. I'd done a lot to earn their respect. But with the professional narc Crosley on our alleged side, how long would it be 'til pigs hauled me in for murder?

As this thought flitted through my mind, the front door banged shut. Boots stomped through the foyer.

"Hunt! Van! This is it! This is the final straw!"

Hunt's nose wrinkled as if he smelled something nasty. "Crosley?"

Before I could say "Unfortunately, yes," Crosley in the flesh strolled into the kitchen.

CHAPTER SEVENTEEN

Hunt

"This is the final fucking straw!" Crosley declared again. Behind him, Pinky peeked around the corner, as if she didn't approve of his actions but was just riding one up with him.

To Crosley's credit, he *did* toss a glance at my distended crotch, but no disapproving or queasy emotion colored his face. He was a hundred ten percent fed up with something. "I *tried* to put down Jackie Daytona, after all the insults he hurled at me!"

Van and I perked up at this. We wanted Jackie Daytona permanently rubbed out, but we would prefer if the instigator were us. I said, "So what happened? We, ah, had to leave early."

Crosley smiled. "Yeah, and what a sight! Van, you're the man! You nailed Tyrone Assclown right through the amygdala!"

That Crosley would use a word like "amygdala" only distracted me for a split second. As usual, the narc was on to something else now.

"And you saved Rover Florkowski from Needle Dick Nick! Dick's throat wound up all over the back of Squee's cut, and now Rover is your buddy for life."

At this, Van finally stood. "No!" he protested. "Please tell me no!"

I had to laugh. "It's your heroics, Van. You reap the rewards."

Van flung a hand in the air and moaned. *"Nooo. . ."*

Crosley continued, "And was that you who plugged George Zip? That's what Turk said, you picked him off from around a corner."

Van was so entrenched in his drama, I answered for him. "Yeah. George Zip. Plumb through the heart."

Pinky finally revealed herself to calm down Van. She had to stand on tiptoes to stroke his hair. "It's okay, honeybee. I'll be your bodyguard. I won't let Rover within ten yards of you."

I asked Crosley, "So how did it end? Is Bond OK?"

"Bond was only shot in the bicep. He'll pull through with an awesome scar to tell a story. Lock was bashed pretty good in the skull with a hubcap. We think he has a concussion. Dipstick got brained with a fire extinguisher, and Dr. Moog had a huge chunk of his back ripped open with a mace."

Silence ensued, until I said, "A mace? Like, that medieval club with spikes?"

Crosley pointed at me. "That's the one. But you, Van the Man, you buried more assholes than anyone! Noel picked off PJ. Or Squee. One of them."

I asked, "The priest? Well, listen here, Crosley. The most important thing is, did Daytona get away scot-free?"

"So free of scots his kilt was plain. I shot in his general direction, but only wound up thunking some guy's gas tank. When gasoline started pouring out and covering the parking lot, that's when people finally ran."

"Well," said Pinky, "you shouldn't have been killing anyone, Crosley. That's a distinct parole violation."

"Tell me about it!" cried Crosley. "My P.O. is gonna remand me into custody regardless because I turned on the Baggers, and that's their target. I'm worthless to them without any intel on the Baggers. So listen, Van and Hunt. If I give you one last nugget of knowledge, will you trust me? I want to have one more hurrah before being returned to Utah State."

Naturally we had to know the validity of this nugget before saying yes. Van beat me to it. "Depends on how reliable your dirt is."

Crosley reached into a bowl on the counter, grabbing a carrot. He took one loud crunch out of it. Pebbles of carrot jumbled his words. "Oh, it's reliable all right. Reliable as a chocolate fireman."

Pinky frowned. "But a chocolate fireman would melt—"

Crosley waved half a carrot at her. "Point being, I know for a fact after the rumble, Jackie was going to take the opportunity to ride to the Dead Mountains Wilderness Area to avail his sore back of the hot springs there."

We all looked at him with upraised palms, scrunched shoulders. "And . . . ?"

Crosley looked surreptitiously from side to side, as though more narcs squatted in the next room. When he reached inside his back jeans pocket to withdraw something top secret, we all backed away.

It was only a plastic bottle of Visine. Everyone exhaled loudly.

"*This*," said Mr. Shelvador, "is my secret weapon."

"Weapon?" I quizzed. "In what way?"

Crosley *tsk-tsked* as if we were dense. "I've been putting it in his coffee, in his beer!"

"So *what*?" Pinky yelped. "What the fuck do eyedrops have to do with anything?"

Crosley held the little bottle closer to our eyeballs. "Tetrahydrozoline," he intoned.

I barked, "Gets absorbed through your guts into your blood!"

Van, Pinky, and even Crosley glared at me. Pinky demanded, "I thought you weren't a chemist!"

"I'm *not*," I protested, "but any high school graduate can tell you that. Once it's absorbed, it moves to your heart and central nervous system. Right, Crosley?"

"Right!" said Crosley. "It can cause coma."

I added, "If it drops his body temp, being cold might be more incentive to get into the hot springs."

Crosley looked on with shining eyes. "Where we kill him."

Van sliced the air with his arm. "Where *I* kill him, excuse the fuck out of me!"

Pinky stepped into the referee role. "Can we all agree that whoever kills him gets credit for avenging Van's lover? Shit. You guys act like you're all crack shots. Fact is, it'll be up to whoever has the best sights on the guy. Then Van can begin the healing, as they say. And Crosley. You shouldn't be popping anyone off anyway."

I felt Pinky basically left it up to Van and I to fight it out among ourselves, but she was right. Fate would dictate who buried Daytona.

Pinky declared, "I like what you did with this place, Hunt. You happened to have this furniture lying around? It really fits in with the architecture." She ran a finger along a dust-free Scandinavian sideboard. It was also free of any décor aside from a brandy and a whiskey bottle.

I said, "Yeah, it was lying around my ex-wife's house."

I forgot that this might be a trigger for Van, but he only gave me friendly side-eye, the lopsided grin. I couldn't wait to have his nipple pierced, having seen guys with rings and barbells during my lust scrolling. I'd get on my knees and take it between my teeth and —

"You coming to the hot springs?" he asked me. "I'd rather you not get involved in this whole messy blood feud."

Truth was, I would've loved to go to the hot springs. Maybe it was the murderous side of me finally coming out, the sinister, gangster side I'd last expressed in college. And maybe I wanted to avenge Van myself. I hadn't really done squat during the rumble. "I would, but I'm due back at work tomorrow. The Russians sent off a rocket last month that's scheduled for re-entry and no one knows where."

That grin. That oceanic face. "Good. I don't want this shit on your hands."

"But I want to go. I want to help you avenge Claude."

His eyes sparkled. "The *real* Claude Berger."

It was good we could joke about it now.

Van snapped to attention. "*Mighty!*"

Mighty was meowing at the sliding glass door. I'd left him a tablespoon of wet food before racing off to Kingman and he'd obviously polished that off. All four of us smashed ourselves against the glass door, fingertips, noses and all. Mighty wasn't scared. He looked at us defiantly.

"He's come back to you," Van breathed.

"Yeah," I admitted. "He even let me pet him."

Pinky said, "Well then. Get out there and pet!"

I shoved an unopened can of cat food into Crosley's palm, demanding, "open." I slid the glass door quietly, stepping with light toes onto the patio.

Mighty raced for my ankles, slithering in and around my boots as though he were lacing me together. I led him to his bowl where I'd placed a chair and sat like a spirit, Van tiptoeing behind me. Mighty threaded his flowing body through both of us, and Van breathed,

"He came back. To you."

"To *us*," I affirmed, daring to reach down and pet the cat's spine with wiggling fingers.

Van followed suit and the cat seemed utterly fine with it. It was only when Crosley stepped, albeit lightly, onto the patio that Mighty jumped and ran off a few steps. But when he saw the food, he returned.

"Let me give it," I said, accepting the can and spoon from Crosley. Mighty lapped up the food with a mushy flicking of his tongue. "Winter turns to spring," I quoted from Nichiren, referring to a renewed hope in things.

Van squatted down to pet Mighty with his fingertips. "Pray to the heavenly gods with all your heart. Be diligent in faith so your desire will be fulfilled."

"I think you guys were diligent," Pinky said, somewhere behind us. "And Hunt. I hate to say it. But I think you should accompany Van to the hot springs."

In my heart, I agreed. Maybe the rocket would take its time and hit our planet the next day. Maybe it would plunge into the South China Sea.

Either way, I had to have Van's back when he clashed with his nemesis.

CHAPTER EIGHTEEN

Van

"This is very concerning," said Hunt, kneeling by the saline soaking pond. The beach was a rim of crusty salt that crunched beneath our boots. This particular pond was named The Wizard Pool, according to a hand-embossed sign hammered into the earth. Farther up the washboard road, another sign had intrigued me. "Fled to Dead Mountains from Bishop to die, instead found paradise & pagans, 2018." Apparently back in the day people would ride the dunes naked, a six-shooter in one hand, a beer in the other. Now signs reminded you to wear your lid, alcohol forbidden.

Squatting next to Van, I asked, "What's concerning?"

His fingers dabbled in the water. "This water is easily a hundred and five. That means the source pool, if he's up there, is at least five degrees hotter."

Crosley, looming above us with hands on hips, blurted, "You can't go in the source pool! That's heretical! Everyone knows that!"

We both stared slack-jawed at the clown who never failed to amaze. This encouraged him to add, "That's a no-no on all levels! The source pool supplies water to the other pools, to the kitchen. Contaminating it with your body is ignorant and heathen!"

"Pagan?" I suggested, thinking of the sign.

Crosley pointed at me. "Exactly." I remembered his Mormon background. Maybe it was a traditional Mormon thing, to soak in hot pools.

"Not to mention," said Hunt, rising to a stand, "it's fucking ninety degrees out here, which would really compound any health issues he already has." He looked down at Crosley. "Like Tetrahydrozoline poisoning."

Crosley held up his hands. "Hey. Don't look at me."

Hunt said, "But you're the one who put Visine in his beer."

"Well, yeah. I was squeezing whole squirts in there."

"So you *are* the one I should be looking at."

Remembering Pinky's advice, I stood. "Hey. Whichever way the goon goes is fine with me. Let's head on up to the source pond. Google maps says it's about three miles up."

Hunt rode his own chopper on this journey. I guess there was an unspoken fact-check that if we needed to split up to surround anyone, it'd be best if we all had our own rides. For this outing, he'd chosen incredibly skinny jeans stuffed into his shit-kicking boots, his cock nestled confidently in the crotch. He resembled an *Easy Rider* character in his saddle, holding onto his ape hangers, fringes of his suede jacket rustling in the breeze.

His long, lush hair and round-rimmed shades added to the authentic allure. My backwoods bumpkin had come the long way round to this sea change, and he deserved credit for every tiny struggle he'd overcome. This son of the soil was an outlaw scientist whose scope of reality included entire heavens. I still felt like a nothing next to him, but I was growing. My confidence had risen, thanks to Dr. Mountjoy.

I ran my fingers through his hair before he put on his lid. "Hunt. I want to give you one last chance to cut and run. Crosley's fate is fucked and determined already. He seems to know it, so he's got nothing to lose. Me? It's my honor at stake, my karma."

Hunt nodded grimly. "Not to mention, if you don't do it, they'll do what they did to Claude another time."

"Definitely. But you've got no dog in this fight. And listen, I couldn't bear it if I had to bring your beautiful body back to Rough and Ready in my fucking van. I just couldn't live another day."

Hunt's eyes behind the olive lenses regarded me with sincerity. "And I couldn't live if I wasn't there to help." He placed his palm on my chest. "I should've believed in you from the beginning. I can't take that all back. Y'all were hiding your identity from the Baggers because you intended revenge. Of course you couldn't show your true self in the fucking ethernet. Listen, you raggedy welder. I fucking love the real you. We've tried to hide our true selves from that disapproving world. We suffered in silence."

He sat up straighter, a fresh, promising vibe to his face. "Look. I'm pretty much a crack shot. I've spent years looking through scopes. Who knows? I might surprise you."

I was going to say I believed him, but Crosley was arcing a frantic arm and pointing at the washboard dirt road. "Someone's coming," he mouthed.

Hunt and I tore our eyes away from each other. Yes, farther up toward the source pool came a puff of dust and a remote roar of pipes. Had someone realized you don't disrespect the source, and come back here for a guilt-free soak?

We wouldn't wait to find out.

I leaped into my saddle, waved a wide arm at my men, and roared to the road, timing it so the three of us spread in a barrier, not giving the fucktard time to dart into the dunes. All three of us pulled our pieces and racked in rounds, leveling them at Jackie Daytona's head. That encouraged him to stop.

He wore no lid, and even with both boots on the ground he wobbled like an elephant on ice skates.

I could have buried him then, but I wanted him to suffer.

Hunt

It was the first time I'd ever pointed a gun at a human being.

Sure, in the rumble I'd randomly squeezed the trigger. But I was probably the clem who'd hit the WRONG WAY sign smack in the middle of the *O*. I mean, there was so much crap going on. I acted on emotion, allowing my scientific mind to go blank. I'd determined not to repeat that mistake today.

Van spoke, like a newscaster, true and clear. "Jackie Daytona, we meet again. Funny how you murdered my friend in Hank's Hot Springs and now I get to murder you in a hot spring."

"Let me pass," said Daytona, voice as wobbly as his legs. He glanced at a couple of roving burros, and for a second we could've all plugged him without him even seeing it coming. But I was taking my cue from my lover.

"I don't think so," intoned Van. He waved his piece on a loose wrist. "I want you to get back to that source pool."

"No, no," protested Jackie, eyes hollow in his skull. "That place is . . . bad."

Van chuckled evilly. It was a thrill to see this side of him. "All the more reason to go back. Come on. Get the lead out, you fucking hypocritical pervert."

"Pop a U-ie," commanded Crosley.

"Disarm him," I suggested to Van.

Van nodded and dismounted. He kept his iron raised like the angry white man who had overtaken his soul. He whipped the piece from Daytona's waistband, wedging it into his own, and felt Daytona's boots for concealed weapons. Checking the saddlebags, Van tossed a daypack that probably contained drugs into a dry wash. He could care less if Daytona's identity was revealed to the pigs.

He nodded once again. "All right. Ride."

We rumbled up the corrugated road. I wondered why the Society's Bagger called the source pool bad. Was it for the same reasons Crosley noted? The sanctity of the pond, honoring the art installations, dishwashing stations, lawns and palm trees planted over the decades? Charles Manson was alleged to have visited here back in the heyday, maybe lending it that ominous yet light-hearted vibe.

The mountains framing us were composed of dark volcanic ash. Lengthening shadows by the setting sun brought steep garnet slopes and washes into sharp focus. One slope was different. It resembled an enormous pumpkin, bursting with stormy mint green water. I swung an arm at Van, who rode in the middle — I wanted him to detour. He acknowledged me with a clenched jaw and nod, but he made no motion to take my advice. He was one determined man. I needed to respect that.

The final thermal spring sat in the shadow of the black mountain slab. Members of the springs community had encircled it with boulders as large as they could lift, and someone had stuck a hand-carved sign in the rocks. *Source pool.*

Before we thundered to a stop, I knew something was vastly fucked, in a horror movie way.

A body already floated facedown in the pool.

Clutching our irons, we dismounted, riveted to the *thing* ebbing and flowing. I glanced at Daytona and thought I saw dismay. His Victorian 'do curling around his jaw, his mouth formed an upside-down U, like an actor in a bad historical. Even his leather cut made him resemble a man about town as he too staggered in shock toward the short rock wall.

Crosley waved his gun at Daytona. "Who the fuck is that? Looks like Squee!"

The Jane Austen hero was slack-jawed. "I . . . I . . . "

Van seemed brimming with glee. "Well, *bless your heart,* you ever-lovin' dirtbag! You buried your own fucking man!"

Squee's leather jacket complete with Society's Bag backpatch squished aside to reveal bloated, mossy green flesh. I wouldn't have recognized him, but Crosley seemed genuinely distraught.

"What the fuck, Jackie?" Crosley cried, advancing on his former Sergeant-at-Arms. "Why'd you fucking kill Squee? Because he didn't have rope for his mattress?"

Jackie's mouth was an *O.* "I . . . I didn't do it! I swear!"

Crosley demanded, "Then how'd he get there, all . . . " Glancing at the body, Crosley tried to find his words.

Skin had begun separating from Squee's hands like he wore gloves. The funk of bodily gas wafted over us, making me wonder how long the guy'd been there. So difficult to describe the stench of a body—a pile of rancid striped bass, month-old dead rats under your deck, or more accurately, someone who hadn't bathed in a month.

Van filled in for Crosley. "All bloated and decomposing? When did you get here?"

Daytona wiped his face as though to cleanse it of the decomp. "Uh . . . yesterday, I think . . . Squee and Gangbang Greg were drinking my health tea. Greg went wandering off into the desert like on a vision quest, and Squee, uh . . . "

I queried, "Health tea? What's in it?"

Daytona shrugged, as though three guns weren't trained on him and he were in a harmless nightmare. We were just symbolic representations of parts of his psyche, and he couldn't analyze the hieroglyphics of our talk. "Hell if I know. Crosley here makes it for me."

Van and I looked to Crosley. "Health tea?" we both uttered.

Crosley had no answer for that one. It was evident his tampering with eye drops had already killed Squee, a guy he seemed to have no beef with. I was all for hurrying along the demise of the two-faced closeted assmuncher with pursed Victorian lips, but a new scene burst upon us.

Another Bagger, perhaps Gangbang Greg, ran over the sandy rise flailing his arms. Shirtless, he seemed to have already decomposed, his blubbering stomach marbled with veins the shade of mulled wine. It was like he'd started to rot from the inside out.

"Antifa is coming!" it sounded like he said. "They're coming to undermine the John Birch Society!"

What in the name of sweet breakfast meats was this guy burbling?

Jackie Daytona put out calming hands. "It's okay, Greg. Remember I told you, antifa isn't a real thing. And the thing about babies in a pizza parlor isn't true, either."

Gangbang Greg didn't seem to care about reality. His teeth were really, really moldy. I imagined I could smell him from twenty yards away, but it was probably dead old Squee. "The cabal is going to Guantanamo Bay! This is the calm before the storm and we have to get ready!"

Daytona started to say, "That's fine, Greg. But right now we need to—"

In a flash Greg withdrew a piece and shot it in our direction. He hit some limestone slope behind us, and my peripheral vision filled with flying powder.

My animal instincts kicked in, and I shot back. Funny, I remember Van giving me some serious side-eye, but I wouldn't relent. Darting to the right of Daytona, I again shot at Gangbang Greg, who scooted behind a palm tree after squeezing off a round that flew wide by about five yards. I was racing *into* his line of fire, as all the mechanisms of physics were laid clear to me. My long legs would carry me down the gulley and soon I'd have a clean line of sight to Greg.

"Hunt, stop!" yelled Van, but he was firing rounds at the palm tree, too.

Chunks of fibrous tree trunk flew in all directions, and Greg still sashayed his pendulous stomach to and fro, failing to hide his obvious silhouette. Another couple bullets and I only shot more woody mulch off the tree. The farther right I circled, the farther counter-clockwise Greg coiled around the trunk, now yelling, "JFK Junior is still alive!"

If I didn't nail this nozzle, Van would, and I wanted to display my loyalty to him. I shouted, "Shut the fuck up, or I'll send space lasers to murder your club!"

That actually seemed to work for a split second. The demented guy high on Visine paused while I took a few more strategic, silent steps.

Peeking his head from behind the trunk, he said, "Really? How does that work? Do you set a wildfire first, or burn our encampment—"

Pow. I nailed the guy so accurately in the forehead, white pieces of parietal bone spewed in a fan along with various other oral structures. My iron seemed to vibrate in my hand as I finally lowered it. Gangbang Greg, missing half his skull, slumped to the sand.

My mission was complete.

I knew there was no time to analyze anything. I turned to Van, who now wore the same slack-jawed look of awe as Daytona. "Van!" I yelled, to snap him out of it. "Did you see that pool we passed by, chartreuse water?"

"Yeah!" replied Crosley, chipper as always. "It looked like a pumpkin!"

"Exactly."

"Kind of seafoam, mint-colored water," he added, all artistic, maybe thinking of his Crayolas.

I said, "We need to get Daytona here into that pond. Believe me. Then we can all take pride in his demise."

"Got you," said Van, once again in charge of the scene. He yelled at Daytona, "Hey. The doctor here has a prescription for you."

Jackie seemed to genuinely take the man on a literal level. His face even lifted a shade. "Really? To help my back? Some new drug?"

Van shrugged. "In a way." Waggling his piece at the Sergeant-at-Arms, Van ordered him to mount his ride.

Before we started our scoots, I gave a nod to my lover. "Good going."

He smiled with stars in his eyes. "I should say that to you. Good show on Gangbang Greg."

I shrugged it off. "I was just protecting you." My next statement took me by surprise. "Protecting the club."

I had no idea the extent to which I already felt part of the club. Not only were we defeating Van's intensely personal enemy, we were defending the club—our new family.

A new pride swelled in my chest as we started back to the pumpkin pool.

Van

I trusted my stargazing friend.

I can't explain how alluring—exciting, stimulating even—it felt to watch Hunt pick off that lubbering old fool. It was as though we told them there's a new boss in town. I saw the mathematical equations Hunt calculated as he circled that dotard, hunting him like a coyote. Still, it was a shocker to see him blow that guy's head clean off. Being a stargazer, he probably hadn't had much experience with the insides of folks' bodies. Yet his face was solid as a monument in the aftermath.

So when Hunt practically ordered me to get Jackie Daytona into that pumpkin-shaped pond, I took him at his word. There was something special about the minty water, maybe poisoned with some heavy metals. Being a welder let me know it might be churning with copper or lead. In fact, there was no road, even a washboard one, heading to the pumpkin formation. We had to fake it, circling around some cholla cacti, Daytona wobblier than ever. Crosley had assisted me with his Visine poisoning, but I wanted to finish that fucker off myself.

One item that came from yonder was a Jeep type truck heading against our traffic. It was getting too dark to see who drove, and there was no writing on the door, but he headed for the Revenge Pool we'd just come from. I fixed to make this a speedy deal and be done with it.

"Look, Jackie," I called when all our engines were stilled. I waved my Beretta to move him to the enormous squash, just oozing and spilling metallic beauty. "This here pool's the end of the line for the likes of you. Consider it your last bath before you pay the price for killing my friend in Hank's Hot Springs."

Jackie screwed up his annoying face. "What do you keep yammering about Hank's Hot Springs?"

Rage boiled in the pit of my stomach, like a knife stabbing my gut. "It was you who beat him to death outside the gay club, once you were finished ogling and fondling all the twinks."

"What? In North Carolina?" Daytona glanced at the pumpkin. He even chuckled a little! "Sure, we were there a year ago or so. Don't remember much of what we did. I was so hammered the whole time, back when I thought booze would help my back."

I took a few steps closer to that vile person. "We saw you in the club grabbing guys between the legs. You, Tyrone, PJ, Squee, Gangbang—"

Jackie thrust his lower jaw at me. "Why would we do that? Fags are despicable. You disgusting Bent Zealots just live to suck dick."

"In your dreams," said Crosley. He wasn't gay but he sure stood up for us.

Louder, I yelled, "Oh *yeah*? I suppose you forget Marcel and the red wings club?"

Daytona snorted. How was it possible for him to look so superior with three barrels trained on him? "Marcel? You mean that woman I was forced to lick to gain entry into the red wings club? What did she have to do with anyone being gay?"

I was dumbstruck. He lied like a corrupt politician—recasting history, playing innocent. I remembered that most of the men witness to his twisted oral sex had now gone to the place in the sky. I shouted at Crosley from the corner of my mouth. "Do you believe this fucker? Not only was he sucking dick, he was *eager* about it, completely *into* it — "

"Life is supposed to teach you, and you haven't learned a damned thing from it!" Crosley bridged the gap between himself and Daytona with a few long strides. I almost felt personal satisfaction when he pistol-whipped the colossal asswad across the cheekbone. Daytona flailed backward, nearly stumbling over his own boots. "God is going to punish you for all your mistakes! You're supposed to be on a road to moral growth and betterment, not going down a pisshole lying about not liking dick!"

Crosley's Mormon speech encouraged me. "Be true to your own nature, however warped you think it is, like Hunt and I have! Hiding and lying twists your fucking spirit, you skidmark."

Daytona was having none of our righteous lecturing. I didn't expect him to have a revelation, but I also didn't expect him to jump right back into the depraved Society's Bagger logic and convoluted reasoning. With a foggy bruise already forming on his cheek, Daytona railed. "You cocksuckers think everyone should be the same as you, and *like* you! What if we were raised to know your homosexual agenda was poisoning the minds of our children?"

I glanced at Hunt. I knew his mother spouted those theories. His jaw twitched with fury.

I yelled, "That's your fucking problem! We were open to changing our minds, to improving our lives, not living underground, hiding and pretending. We both saw you suck that guy's dick with total excitement and craving, and you can't even admit it!"

To his credit, Jackie faced me head-on. Either he was too high to give a shit about dying, or he welcomed it. Behind him the pumpkin overflowed with turquoise water I was now convinced was churning with arsenic. Hunt knew his stuff.

"Gays molest children. Two men married together rot and pervert our children. Now they're infiltrating our military —"

I shot Daytona in the leg.

I knew you're supposed to only squeeze off the kill shot. Shoot to kill, not maim. Otherwise what are you standing there for? I just didn't want to hear his whacked rant any longer, and it worked. Wincing almost doubled over, Daytona held his leg and glared at me.

"How fucking dare —"

He started his sentence, but I finished it. "How dare I force you into that pool? Move it, Daytona. We're burning daylight. You killed Claude Berger in Hank's Hot Springs and now I'm burying you in the Dead Mountains hot springs."

Hunt and Crosley joined me in rustling the dickwipe into the pool. With our barrels pressed to his back and shoulders we shoved him into the metallic water. He went like a guy stepping in a poo minefield, lifting his feet high. Without remorse until the bitter end!

"You — you fuckers — are all mentally ill drug addicts!"

"Oh *yeah*?" sneered Hunt. "Like *you*?"

Daytona sputtered, unable to think of a comeback. He only went into the pool to his waist, arms held up as though he gripped a ballet skirt. He seemed very injured and victimized by homosexuals in general. What had happened to twist such a person? I didn't care. I tried to poke him further, but I'd of had to put my boots into the boiling water too.

Crosley must've noticed, for he said, "I'll get in on the other side. We'll shoot him 'til he's up to his neck."

He high-stepped it over to the other side while yelling psychoanalytical Mormon stuff at Daytona. "You feel no guilt for what you've done, how many people you've murdered, proof you're a narcissistic sociopath! Yeah, I studied that at Brigham Young. I was gonna be a criminal analyst until my mother-in-law fucked it up. Another narcissistic sociopath! When normal people like us sin, we feel guilt and pain. You created your own conditions of your life, Jackie. The gift of agency means we create our own reality. Oh, what the fuck is this?"

Hunt and I looked at each other. We were almost smiling! I'd never seen Hunt look so carefree, yet overflowing with anger at the same time. It was like the rage energized him, moved him forward.

Then we frowned, because it looked like Crosley was stuck in some mud. He really couldn't seem to lift his boots. He gripped one leg and tried to pull. Nothing.

"What is it, Crosley?" I yelled, striding around the pool to view his dilemma.

"It—it seems like fucking *quicksand!*"

"What the hell?" said Hunt, coming around to our side too.

Indeed, Crosley had stepped into a little beach that had instantly engulfed his ankles with gritty clay. It really *did* look like quicksand!

"What the fuck?" I said, while Hunt leaped into action doing something in the nearby scrub bushes. "Wait—I've heard this on TV—don't struggle."

Crosley cried, "Then how the fuck do I get out of here?"

That was a good point. To make matters fucking worse, Daytona picked this moment to blurt his whacked theories.

"See, Shelvador? It's your God taking vengeance on you for torturing me like this! He's telling you 'Look, asshole, this is what you get for harassing the Sergeant-at-Arms of Society's Baggers! This'll show you, you dimwitted halfwitted screwball—*whoa.*"

Daytona wavered in the water. He seemed to be trying to hold himself up with his palms on the surface of the pool. Was he getting sucked into quicksand, too? No, it must've been the arsenic lacing the water getting to him. He toppled over like a palm made of mud in the liquid.

He still burbled. "Gays . . . you could be straight if you wanted to . . . "

I'd had enough. I shot him through the forehead, the bullet going through the skull and embedding itself somewhere in the limestone depths. Just a tiny bloom of scarlet red emanated from his forehead, swirling into a gorgeous painting before being swept away.

It was freeing. I shoved my piece into my waistband, glad I could now use both hands for other things. Hunt emerged from the bush with a long stick of some kind. Looked like a trunk from a chapparal yucca, six feet tall and sprouting white bell-shaped flowers. I knew those pointy leaves could be painful, but we didn't have much other choice.

"Give me your piece," I said, because I saw in my peripheral vision a flashing orange light, like on the cab of a ranger's truck, heading toward the source pool. There was an emergency, maybe when the Jeep guy found those bodies poisoning his beloved pool. I was able to grab Crosley's iron just as Hunt slapped the yucca trunk onto the sand in front him. The Mormon narc was now up to his knees, as Hunt instructed,

"Don't move. As slowly as you can, flop onto your back."

Crosley did as ordered, but he'd apparently seen the light too—or heard it when the ranger used his speaker. The guy sounded like Peanuts adults, blaring a mumble of instructions. Crosley said, "You guys go. Save your asses. You shouldn't have to pay for any of this. This is your divine retribution."

Hunt kept saying, "Are you stable on your back? Drop onto your back on top of that yucca pole."

Crosley flopped, yet he kept insisting, "Go, you guys! Go! I'm serious as taxes! This is my fate. Take my piece—I don't need a weapons charge on top of everything else."

Like . . . dead bodies? I said, "How're you going to explain this, Crosley? There are three buried people."

"Don't worry, I won't implicate you. As long as you split, leave, *go!*"

Hunt said, "Good. Rest the pole under your hips as you pull out your feet."

Crosley stuttered, "I will! Just go, go, *go*! I needed one last hurrah and I got it, so *go!*"

Hands on hips, Hunt glanced at me. His eyes seemed to be saying yes. *Yes, let's go. You don't need to pay for getting revenge for Claude.*

As much as it ran against my grain to leave a man behind, Crosley was right. He'd already accepted he was going back to Utah State. The less people implicated in our blood feud, the better. Besides, there was a chance he could get out of the hole before the ranger came back, or sent a real cop. The closest real pig was probably an hour away in Needles.

I saluted Crosley as he moved his body atop the yucca trunk. "You're the man, Crosley Shelvador." Never thought I'd be saying those words, but they were heartfelt.

Hunt saluted too. "Be right behind us. Ride sweep."

Ride sweep. That's what I'd been doing my whole life, riding tail gunner, bringing up the rear, acting like a sideshow to my own life. Now I was top gun, in control.

We took our leave of our struggling companion sort of sedately. We didn't thrash it or look any more suspicious than we already were. We just rumbled, side by side. Evils may have been piling up, but they can't win out against a simple great truth. Lots of raging fires are quenched by a single rain shower.

That was Hunt and me—a great cleansing rainstorm.

Rain on me. I could handle it now.

We passed a cop car with flashing lights as it headed toward the source pool.

EPILOGUE

"Maybe tomorrow…
Maybe tonight
I've built a castle around
My hollow fright… "
My own corny college lyrics came back to haunt me.

I hustled about the Happy Hour clubhouse like a good Prospect. Being Lock's thirty-sixth birthday, there was a big to-do that day, and I could only participate in an underling capacity. I wore my plain black leather cut, not allowed to even sew on the Filthy Few patch they all agreed I'd earned.

Oh, I was allowed to wear a black and white PROSPECT patch.

As the party built steam, some asswipe decided it'd be witty to play an old CD of my Princeton band, Great Caeser's Ghost. I strode around, threading between solid, hairy bikers like they were buoys in a waterskiing course, carrying dishes and glasses and, if the club member was Rover, a used condom to dispose of. On top of this shame, I was forced to listen to myself wailing angst-filled lyrics such as

"I'm just one or two tears and a couple of changes behind you

And I don't know all that much I think I do

So I go running out in search of the perfect stranger

Who'll never make me feel the way you do. . . "
It was one of the disgraceful initiation rites they made me endure.

"Do I sound fat?" I asked Pinky, who was bartending.

She wrinkled her nose while pouring a craft beer for Anson. "What?"

"My singing. On this song. You said I sound fat, like Barry White."

"Ha!" Pinky had to laugh. She resembled a little sprite with pointed ears when she did that. My realtor was also one of my best friends. "Could be. Not that there's anything wrong with that. You've got a resonant, gritty basso profundo. Then you see it's coming from a scarecrow like you."

"Hey," I protested, swiping up Anson's old empty glass.

Pinky jammed her fist onto her hip. "Okay, I'll bite. Muscle bunny."

"That's better."

"And someone's been texting you like mad." She nodded her head at my crotch.

Mortified yet grinning, I slunk back to the kitchen. I placed the beer glasses by the sink with the other dishes I was supposed to wash. I'd always been pretty clean in college, not like those students with a truckload of Starbucks cups and overflowing ashtrays. Or an unframed torn Queen poster, as Van had weirdly put up in our workout room. He said it gave him inspiration, and I assumed it was Mercury's queerness, although had Freddie ever come out of the closet?

But when I moved to yank my phone from my pocket, there was Rover, close enough to use the same toothpick.

"Shake it, sweet cheeks." He even squeezed my ass this time.

I lifted my upper lip at him, but didn't dare say a word. I had to replace the phone and walk away from the disgusting biker. I crammed my way past the Navajo kid flipping burgers, Brick Mantooth. He worked making shatter with a few other Native American youths at Herbal Legends, the weed op run by Turk. Someone told me they'd literally been saved by the club from enslavement, chained to a meth-making trailer.

"*Sih-kiss.*" Brick called me "friend" in his Diné language. "I need more clean griddle pans. And your buddy there needs clean salad bowls."

"On it," I said automatically, glad to put a couple bodies between Rover and myself. Now he had his head stuck in the big fridge, cramming a raw hot dog into his chops.

I shivered, my cock expanding as I brushed past Van's ass, cubing and dicing radishes and cheese. He too returned his phone to his pocket, just in time for mine to chime again.

"Asshole," I breathed against his ear. His barbell-pierced nipple under the tight muscle shirt was screaming for a pinch, but there was no time. I had to shove my hands into soapy water and wash pots and pans.

Holding my phone to the window that looked onto the alley, I thumbed through the recent texts.

Take out your cock and send me a photo.

I want one soft. One after you stroke yourself. One of your massive erection and balls full of jizz.

Unbuttoning my prick with my back to a party of bikers was the lewdest, erotic, kinky thing I'd ever done—and I was loving it. Placing my swelling cock on the cool metal of the sink, I snatched a few photos for Van. In the bar area drunken slurring men started a rousing version of "Happy Birthday" for Lock. From the corner of my eye I saw Rover heading my way, and I managed to cram my cock back under my dishwasher's apron and shove a few pans into the sink.

Working laser fast, my hands blurred as I swiped my sponge. *Happy Birthday, dear fuckwad. Happy Birthday, dear dirtbag. Happy Birthday, dear Veep. Happy Birthday to yooo . . .*

Where was Rover? I faced a wall, and there was nowhere else for him to go. He had to be heading for me. Finally the suspense was too much, and I looked over my shoulder. *Damnation.* He was manhandling my man, SoulWrestler.

Van's hard grimace showed his irritation, and I reacted with instinct.

"Hey!" I yelled across the noisy, clattering room. "Get your hands off him *now!*"

Rover's hand on Van's ass froze. I wondered what the fuck words he'd been sniveling into Van's ear. *Bless my heart. I'm holding a cleaver.*

No wonder Rover backed away slowly, hands up. Van, meanwhile, exploded in laughter. My jaw dropped as I lowered my dripping weapon.

"Prospect," Brick shouted out. "We want tomato ketchup for these burgers, not blood."

No matter that Brick was fifteen years younger than me. I had to lower the cleaver. Van and I shared grins that we accepted each other, no matter how crazy, subservient, or passionate we could be. I'd never accepted myself before Van. If I didn't love myself, how did I expect others to?

I turned back to my dishes, but in between I snuck a look at my new text.

Do you want to touch yourself? Show me your hand down your pants.

Like a true sub, I was about to comply when an entire herd of bikers came tumbling into the kitchen.

"Go for it!" they urged someone.

"Yeah! Do it!"

"Let's see some skin!"

What tradition was this? A couple of men with heavily patched cuts were the center of attention. Turned out Turk and Lock had clutched in a spontaneous embrace, maybe to show their devotion. What a sight! The Prez and his Veep were in a tongue-filled clutch such as I'd never seen them before. These two Aztec gods were going hard at it, Lock pressing Turk back against a counter where little tamales had been carefully placed. Cornmeal squished out from behind Turk's cut as they made out like teens at the submarine races.

It turned me on, too. Giddy grins decorated everyone's faces. I shoved a bunch of wet dishes into the drying rack and wiped my hands on my apron. *Now.*

Now is the time for action.

Whipping out my phone, I texted Van, who was standing just fifteen yards away, tossing salad fixings into various bowls like he was in a contest.

I've got a surprise. It's waiting in the men's room.

"Emergency," I yelled into Brick's ear as I sideswiped him.

And it was. The biggest emergency of my life. I *needed* Van right now.

The men's room was locked. I banged with my fists on it, but no one yelled from inside. A solution was made plain when Pinky exited the women's room, face wreathed in a grin.

She yanked a thumb at the kitchen. "Sounds like they're even heavier than usual. I've never seen two lovebirds like that."

"Oh *yeah?*" I challenged, just as Van came whipping around the corner. Reaching a hand out to him, we flowed like the tide into the women's, both fumbling to lock the door behind us.

Van was on me like voodoo, stripping my apron, my cut, then my shirt. Tossing them all into the sink, he pressed me back against the vanity, slurping a nipple into his mouth.

"StarGazer," he groaned. "I've got a hankering for you."

"SoulWrestler." I had a handful of his hair, trying to yank his face back so I could kiss him. But his little nibbles made me want to squirt.

We'd come so far, Van and I. We had vast storehouses of treasure in our bodies. But the treasures of the heart were most valuable of all.

Van

Believe me, I've never thrown salad fixings together as fast as I did.

First the seductive texts I sent Hunt, some inspired by the melodramatic yet inspiring lyrics my man had written twenty years earlier. Deathless prose such as

"I've just kicked back for the night don't you know

Cuddled up tight, hear the north wind blow . . . "

spurred me on, exciting me to seductive prose myself. It had actually been Pinky's idea to hand the CD of Princeton hits to DJ Fremont, who busted a gut laughing before he even spun the disc. First I made finger tamales, later massive salads, all while standing at the same station observing Hunt pacing to and fro. He got way more exercise than me zooming from one side of the building to the other, long legs striding, beautiful arms enfolding a clutter of different used dishes.

"Screaming for mercy

It's not the telephone wires

It's me

Shock therapy

Vicious circles

Primal scream

Scream

Scream . . . "

Scream Hunt did, riling me to greater heights as I demanded dick pics, arousing myself probably more than him. But I was safe standing behind my chopping block, erection hidden from view. He had to parade in and out, pouring half-eaten nachos and little bowls of salsa into the trash can, grabbing trays of fresh plastic beer mugs to set by Pinky.

Hunt couldn't hide that giant slug of a prick, snuggled in the crotch of his pants. Not velvet today, he'd been wearing these incredibly tight-fitting 501 jeans that must've been custom-shrunk for his colt's legs. This was my view as the uproar in the bar grew to a crescendo. By the time Lock and Turk came rolling into the kitchen in a clutch, my passion had escalated so steeply my hands practically blurred as I minced olives into a paste.

When we tumbled into the women's room—as clean as a pin thanks to Prospect Hunt—I was well nigh ready to assault my lover. Well, I guess that's what I did, after all. We had sex as fast and furious as it came.

"StarGazer," I moaned before slurping his nipple. He yanked at a fistful of my shaggy hair, but my jaws remained clamped to his pebbled flesh. I hugged his steamy thigh to my crotch as I bit down.

It sounded like Hunt was urging, "Do it. Do it. Do it." Or was that just the echo of the Zealots crowding the kitchen?

Their chanting did reverb down the back hallway, hugging my brain, urging me on. I slid my fingers down the small of his back, the rise of his scorching ass nearly burning me. As I stood, I ran my mouth up his throat, past the jumble of necklaces he still wore. A slick obsidian arrowhead almost cut my tongue, and the slow burn of a polished tiger's eye warmed it.

Hunt leaned back onto the sink, one palm on the marble propping him up. I pressed my hard-on against his and dry-humped with full sweeps of my hips as I sucked his lower lip into my mouth.

"Van," he muttered. "Do it."

That was *not* my imagination. We'd been so busy executing chores for the club we barely had time to blow one another in our kitchen. It almost seemed they did it that way on purpose, keeping one tear-assing around 'til midnight, the other taking out the garbage before sunrise.

Knowing what I'd been through prospecting for the Society's Bag, maybe they went easier on me. And knowing my propensity for cooking, they gave me those tasks. I don't know. It wasn't ours to ask. But I'd been out of my mind thinking of penetrating that tight ring. To actually feel myself twitch and expand inside his steamy channel drove me ape. Today, I was the Dom, the top, the commander in charge.

No one had knocked on the door, so I dared to unbutton his jeans, letting his big cock flop out. I wasted no time in kneeling, to slurp up that big tool—to get it nice and wet. I'd swallowed gallons of my lover's seed by this time, and tonight I had a different thing in mind. I nearly twisted his full scrotum as I gave bruising sucks to his dong.

Low rumbles of leonine pleasure rolled through his chest, and I knew he approved of my technique as the roof my mouth slid past his corona. But there was no way to fully engorge myself on that long dick. My mouth smacked and slurped past his taut mushroom cap, leaving plenty of spit.

There. That was enough. Standing, I whipped out my dick. I spread his knees with mine, encouraging him to hop his ass onto the vanity. His sly grin told me he knew what was coming—literally.

I spit one more time into my hand, this time lubing my own cock. "My boy," I murmured.

Hunt draped a loving hand behind my neck. "Fuck me."

I slurped up his luscious mouth as I slid my penis inside him, inch by inch. My nipple barbell grated and mushed just perfectly against his heated chest. I knew when he grinned with eyes nearly crossed that I had breached his sweet spot. Inching in and out, I concentrated rubbing there, and his groans got louder. Gripping his penis, I thumbed the wet hole, slick enough with my spit and his precome. I jacked him with short bursts of energy. I felt the jizz coming out in tiny spurts as his ass clenched my cock.

Oh yeah. He was ready. This cock virgin was about to get a lesson in submission.

My thrusts now came faster, shallower. I didn't realize it was *I* who was at the mercy of his clutching passage, that's how fast I came. I just lost it. It swept me up like a tornado, actually dizzy with overwhelming ecstasy. Shooting into Hunt's tight little hole gave me a full body thrill like no other.

I jerked and lurched like a man electrified. I wasn't even aware he was coming until semen poured over my wrist and his asshole clutched at my squirting dick. When I opened my eyes, the most gorgeous sight greeted me. Hunt, sitting back on splayed hands, thighs wide open, big dick pulsing. Openmouthed, head tossed back, he jetted on his pelvic bone and dribbled down my arm.

Chuckling, I tried to breathe normally. Bending over, I took a few gulps from his cock but I was too out of breath for much oral play. When Hunt opened his eyes they glittered with something like tears. He tried to kiss me but we were both too torn up, his asshole still clenching my cock.

"Hey! That you, Pinky?"

It sounded like Dr. Moog at the door. Hunt and him had been getting along well lately. Sometimes I'd overhear them talking about the hot springs, about the Visine . . . about Jackie Daytona. I hadn't detected any guilt on Hunt's part for his role in the murders. For that's what they were, murder pure and utter.

Hunt and I laughed. We quickly washed our hands, splashed water on our dicks before stuffing them back in.

Moog yelled, "Pinky, if that's you, you served me too many beers. The men's room is jammed."

Hunt talked in a stage whisper. "How are we gonna avoid getting in trouble? There's no window to climb out of."

"Stella?" Moog yelled out the names of some sweetbutts. "Kenna? Fredericka?"

I had a lame-ass story for Moog. I whipped the door open. "Hey, doctor. We had a beer emergency too. Don't tell anyone we were drinking on the job."

Hunt's jaw dropped, as if he couldn't believe I came up with such a feeble excuse. But the doctor, apparently in a rush, herded us back inside the little room and closed the door.

He proceeded to pee as he told us, "I finally got the autopsy report on Daytona. Seems our closeted friend had a giant AIDS dilemma. Would've died of it soon anyway."

We both went "whoa," seemingly for different reasons. Hunt, oddly, seemed chagrined by this news, I guess because AIDS was one of gay men's biggest fears. I, however, didn't care. Daytona deserved the bubonic plague.

I said, "But that can be controlled nowadays with drugs."

His back to us, Moog shrugged. "Seems he didn't want to take that step to admit he was gay. See, there are all sorts of down sides to not being free and honest with life. He could've been saved, if anyone cared enough."

I said, "If he didn't have a bullet through his head."

Moog flushed and elbowed Hunt away from the sink to wash his hands. "Yeah, well. I've heard some intel from Utah State. Seems that your friend Crosley Shelvador took the fall for murdering Daytona. No mention of you. And I guess they were so pleased he basically took out the entire club by pitting us against them, they're only making him serve another six months."

I slapped myself on the forehead. "Holy *shit!* That condom breath took credit for *my* work!"

Moog raised one eyebrow as he snatched some paper towels. "Yeah, well. Would you rather it the other way around?"

Hunt said, "He actually turned out to be a decent guy. Aside from the, you know, killing his mother-in-law part."

Moog shrugged. "Maybe she deserved it. Maybe she was bad at giving head."

I shrugged too. It made sense. "Okay, I better get back to—"

"*Jesus!*" Another leather cut-wearing brute barged in, shoving us asunder in order to reach the toilet where he kneeled, retching. Dipstick Hunziger held on for dear life as he puked, and Pinky followed hot on his heels.

She barked, "He said it was my bloody Mary that made him sick! That's impossible. It's just tomato juice and vodka."

Moog added, "Or a dirty glass."

"Don't look at me!" I tossed my hands up and managed to squish my way into the hallway where more men were stacking up. It seemed that after the show Turk and Lock had displayed, everyone suddenly needed the bathroom, including the Prez and Veep. Guys were piling up toward the ceiling, limbs and fists defining the scene like an abstract painting. They were frantic, too, like there had been an earthquake. Good thing Hobie Cleminshaw wasn't in there, or the whole thing would've wound up in the basement.

I don't know how we did it, but Hunt spirited me away. Maybe our love swept us away on its powerful tide. But next thing I knew, we were in the chapel—the one place we were never allowed, as prospects. The atmosphere was eerie and forbidden, although we'd be true patch holders soon enough. It *was* quiet as a church in there once Hunt slammed the door. The urgent roar of the poor men in the hallway lowered to a dull thunder.

Pressing me against the door, Hunt caressed my forehead, my cheekbones, my jaw. "Love the man, love the club." He referred to the rumble a few feet away. "How'd we wind up here at this exact place and time? We came from the same place, wound up completely different . . . and now . . . "

I grinned. "We find out that we're the same."

We had a few more minutes together, kissing in the chapel. Then we had to get back to work.

THE END

www.laylawolfe.com

Did you like this book? Leave a review, and Layla will be grateful!

ABOUT THE AUTHOR

Bestselling author **Layla Wolfe** likes to bring you alpha males—sometimes two at a time—and the kick-ass women who love them. Her BARE BONES MC series explores the dark, disturbing life of the biker club in Arizona. Her spinoff series THE BENT ZEALOTS MC is a gritty MM saga. She is currently back to working on the next BARE BONES book.

Layla Wolfe is the pen name of multi-published erotic romance author Karen Mercury.

THE BARE BONES MC

1. The Bare Bones
2. Stay Vertical
3. Bad to the Bones
4. Playing with Monsters
5. Have Gun, Will Travel
6. Shelter from the Storm
7. It Takes a Thief
8. Race with the Devil
9. Making His Bones
10. Road Refugees

THE BENT ZEALOTS MC

1. A Dangerous Reality
2. A Gorgeous Mess
3. A Lone Stranger
4. A Wild Wicked Weekend
5. A Cuddly Toy
6. A Mutual Friend
7. A Long Con
8. A Sexy Thing

THE ASSASSINS OF YOUTH MC

Through A Glass Darkly
A Leap In the Dark

STANDALONES

Dynomite: A Stepbrother Cowboy Romance
The Emerald Triangle: A Forbidden Priest Romance

Going for the Gold

1. Working the Lode
2. Either Ore
3. A Good Prospect
4. Sure as Shooting
5. Blowing off Steam
6. The Obedient Servant

WRITING AS KAREN MERCURY:

The Dark Continent

1. The Hinterlands
2. The Four Quarters of the World
3. Strangely Wonderful

How the West Was Done

1. Training Ivy
2. Disorder in the House
3. Cold Steel and Hot Lead
4. Manifested Destiny
5. The Wild Bunch
6. The Importance of Being Serviced

McQueen Was My Valley

1. Something Sinful This Way Comes
2. Woman on Top
3. The Grass is Greener
4. Two Sirs, With Love

Bound to Please

1. Her Master's Choice
2. The Good Switch

The Sunset Palomino Ranch

1. The Sublime Miss Paige
2. The Subject Was Rose
3. The Substantial Gift

Owner of a Lonely Heart

Hells Delight

1. Three Hearts Beat as One
2. Three of a Perfect Pair
3. Three for All
4. Three Times a Lady

Midnight, New Orleans Style

Redemption Song

Hells Delight: Unbridled

1. Two For the Road
2. Two Tickets to Paradise
3. Two Good Men

https://www.bookbub.com/authors/layla-wolfe Follow me on Bookbub

https://www.amazon.com/Layla-Wolfe/e/B00J7EEMMW/ref=dp_byline_cont_pop_ebooks_1 Follow me on Amazon!

http://laylawolfe.com/ Join my newsletter to receive a free book!

https://www.instagram.com/layla_wolfe/?hl=en Follow me on Instagram!